# DUMBO

Based on Walt Disney Productions'
full-length cartoon feature film

This adaptation by
Derry Moffatt

**NEW ENGLISH LIBRARY**
TIMES MIRROR

Other stories from Disney cartoon feature films
and available in the NEL series

LADY AND THE TRAMP

SNOW WHITE AND THE SEVEN DWARFS

SONG OF THE SOUTH

SLEEPING BEAUTY

ROBIN HOOD

PINOCCHIO

© Walt Disney Productions

FIRST NEL PAPERBACK EDITION SEPTEMBER 1975
Reprinted October 1975

NEL Books are published by
New English Library Limited from Barnard's Inn,
Holborn, London E.C.1.
Made and printed in Great Britain by
Hunt Barnard Printing Ltd, Aylesbury, Bucks.
Typesetting by The Yale Press Ltd, London SE25

45002688 4

# DUMBO

Massive dark clouds hurried across a wintry sky, driven by an icy wind. Snow fell in flurries over the countryside and houses and fields were blanketed beneath a deep, white carpet. Except for the sighing and gusting of the wind, all sounds were muffled. People had eagerly sought the shelter of their homes; cattle and sheep huddled together for warmth in great barns and birds crouched low in their nests.

On this particular cold snowy night, one group of storks were willing to brave the elements. Perched on a billowing cloud, they prepared to take flight. Each of them carried a parachute with a small bundle attached, for the storks were members of the all-important 'Baby Delivery Service.' Their work carried them to every part of the globe: across vast seas, to jungles, deserts, cities, tiny villages and the lonely countryside.

Now, balanced on a raggedy purple cloud they were ready to make a very special 'country' delivery. Their leader glanced round. 'Ready, fellas?' he asked the other storks.

They nodded, fluttering their strong wings. 'The sooner we take off, the better,' answered one. 'My little charge is getting impatient.'

'Right! Away we go!' The leader glided forward and the other birds followed in formation, carefully balancing the precious bundles in their long, powerful beaks. As they flew through the icy air, a song was borne on the wind ... the 'Stork Song'.

Through the snow and sleet and hail,
Through the blizzards — through the gales,
Through the wind and through the rain,
Over the mountains — over plain,
Through the blinding lightning flash
And the mighty thunder crash,
Ever faithful, ever true,
Nothing stops him, he'll get through!
Look out for Mr Stork, that persevering chap,
He'll come along and drop a bundle in your lap.
You may be poor or rich,
It doesn't matter which,
Millionaires ... they get theirs,
Like the butcher and the baker,
So look out for Mr Stork, and let me tell you,
friend,
Don't try to get away, he'll find you in the end;
He'll spot you out in China or he'll fly to
County Cork,
So you'd better look out for Mr Stork!

As the song ended one of the storks called, 'See you later, boys. I've an appointment below.' Swooping, he vanished from sight.

The leader glanced around. 'Keep your eyes open, fellas. We must be getting pretty close now.'

'I see it . . . I see it!' squawked one bird excitedly. 'Look! Over to the right!'

All the birds focused sharp eyes on a large group of buildings brilliantly lit with a variety of coloured lights. A neon sign read, 'The Circus — Winter Quarters.'

'Ah,' nodded the leader, 'we've lots of deliveries for them tonight. Careful fellas . . . no mix-ups now.'

With good-natured chuckles the birds veered off in varying directions. The circus was spread over a vast area and the bears, lions and tigers had their quarters some distance from the giraffes and kangaroos. Soon the air was full of tiny bundles drifting earthwards.

Mrs Bear lay snugly curled up in the corner of her cage. She was fast asleep and a happy grin creased her face for she was dreaming that she had a tiny baby bear. It was a dream that she often had nowadays and waking up always proved to be a big disappointment. Suddenly, something tickled her big toe and she opened her eyes. She blinked rapidly . . . could it be true? A tiny baby bear sat at her feet, his thick brown coat silky as down. Leaning over she picked him up and lovingly licked his teddy bear face, cuddling him close. At last . . . at long last, her dream had come true. But there was yet another surprise in store. A brown ball came rolling across the centre of her cage, closer and closer. Suddenly it stopped spinning at her feet and a tiny creature uncurled itself, shook its head and grinned mischeviously up at her. It was a second bear cub. Mrs Bear could hardly believe her good fortune. Beaming happily, she leaned over and picked up her second baby, then caressed and fondled them both.

Some distance away in another part of the circus, Mrs Kangaroo was leaning against a pile of hay. The cold weather had made her drowsy and she was considering whether to take a nap or to have a snack when a bundle floated right in front of her. To her amazement a baby kangaroo detached himself from a shiny white parachute and hopped through

the air right into her pouch. She smiled adoringly at her new offspring. The stork who had delivered the baby grinned widely. 'Another satisfied customer,' he commented before flying rapidly into the night.

In the pool, a bulky hippopotamus lay on a bed of mud, sending masses of bubbles to the surface of the water. One bubble, much larger than the rest, floated down instead of up. 'That's going the wrong way,' thought the hippo, but when the bubble burst and a tiny hippo swam across the pool, she snorted with pride.

Baby deliveries were going on all over the circus . . . it was proving a very busy night for the storks. Two baby tiger cubs leapt from their bundles and snuggled close to their mother. Their father, pacing the cage in a state of anxiety saw them and all at once he relaxed, smiling with pride at his new family. A baby giraffe drifted earthwards, his parachute narrowly missing a tree. A gust of wind saved what could have been an unhappy plight and the thin, leggy baby wobbled uncertainly towards his mother. With love in her eyes she fondled him and removed the parachute still draped over his back.

In the elephant house, Mrs Jumbo anxiously scanned the skies. For several days she had been expecting Mr Stork to pay her a visit. Through the feathery snowflakes she spotted several small bundles drifting towards her. She raised her trunk in greeting. The stinging wind carried a song to her ears and she listened attentively.

Look out for Mr. Stork,
He's got you on his list,
And when he comes around,
It's useless to resist!
Remember those quintuplets
And the woman in the shoe,
Maybe he's got . . .
His eye on you!

Mrs Jumbo's eyes, black and shiny as buttons, gleamed with hope. But the nearest bundle dropped into a pen on the left. Surely the next one would be for her! But no . . . that blew over to her right. Looking very disappointed, she gazed skyward again . . . but there were no more bundles in sight, only snowflakes dancing in the air. The storks, in formation again, were heading away from the camp, their deliveries made. Sadly, she lowered her trunk and her head drooped. It was not her turn today, after all. Wearing a woebegone expression, she retired to the corner of her pen.

A week had passed since the mass delivery of babies to the circus. Excitement hung in the air, for the time had come for the circus to move to new quarters. Getting the animals and equipment aboard Casey Junior was a mammoth undertaking for the circus folk. Casey Junior, a proud, dependable train with a shiny red engine, was very strong.

It puffed, snorted and tugged its way across the vast American continent and loved every minute of its numerous journeys.

Mrs Jumbo walked beside the tracks to her compartment on the train. So far, the stork had not brought her a precious baby bundle. She frowned. Surely he couldn't have forgotten! Sighing, she lifted her trunk in the air, hoping he would know she had changed her address. It was so worrisome.

The air had a fresh, green scent. Soon, it would be spring and buds would pierce the trees like tiny ears, listening for the warm west wind. Birds would build new nests and fill the world with song . . . but would she, Mrs Jumbo, have a fine, handsome baby to love?

Horses, kangaroos, zebras, lions and tigers, accompanied by their tiny offspring, were herded aboard the train and checked into their various sections. Mrs Jumbo glanced over her shoulder and even though she wasn't feeling happy, she couldn't resist a smile. The two adult giraffes had their long necks craned through holes in the roof of their car and even giraffe junior's head was showing.

'Over here, Mrs Jumbo . . . come along,' called one of the men. 'Lately, you always appear to be in a day-dream.' She joined several other elephants walking up a ramp. Just in case . . . she gave a final glance at the sky. Dusk was falling and there wasn't a sign of a stork. The elephant following Mrs Jumbo tapped her on the back with its trunk. Mrs Jumbo moved forward and finally they were all inside, although the last elephant aboard was hanging over the edge. One of the men gave her bottom a push. Indignantly, she turned to glare at the offender but he shut the door in her face.

'All aboard . . . all aboard!' The ringmaster's authoritative voice carried the length of the train. 'All aboard . . . let's go!' He cracked the ground with his whip and jumped into a compartment. The valiant train steamed and puffed . . . puffed and steamed. It was no easy job to start. At the rear, several cars crashed together. Casey Junior emitted a thin, high squeal and finally managed to move forward. Presently, the circus train and its occupants were gliding across the countryside and, as they travelled, the rhythm of the wheels sang a happy song:

> Casey Junior's coming down the track,
> Coming down the track . . .
> With a smoky stack . . .
> Hear him puffing,
> Coming round the hill,
> Casey's here to thrill
> Every Jack and Jill . . .

The train continued its journey, smoke blowing from its stack as it entered a tunnel going right through the heart of a mountain. As it came out on the other side, the catchy song continued:

> Every time his funny little whistle sounds,
> Everybody hurries to the circus grounds.
> Time for lemonade and crackerjack,
> Casey Junior's back . . .
> Casey Junior's back!

High up in the sky, way above the clouds, a rather breathless stork had lost his way. On his head he wore a peaked hat with bold lettering across the front: 'Baby Delivery Service.' In his beak he held a very rounded bundle. 'Uff!' he said breathlessly. 'I need a rest. I'm exhausted.' Spotting a small fluffy cloud directly below, he dropped his bundle on to its cotton-wool surface and then hopped on himself. Taking a handkerchief from his vest pocket, he mopped his brow. 'My . . . my! Now let me see! Must be right around here somewhere!' He peered over the edge of the cloud, looking earthwards. 'Leastways, I hope it is,' he added.

The round bundle began to slip through a hole in the cloud. 'Whoops!' he cried. 'Ah . . . watch it there!' Diving hastily, he caught it then sat on a firmer cloud. Taking a map from another pocket he turned it over, searching for his route. 'Mmmmm . . . where are we? Here

. . . oh here, Highway 61, four miles to the petrol station. I make a left turn . . .' He flipped his right wing in the air, then paused. From far below came the shrill screech of a train whistle. The stork leaned over the edge of the cloud. 'Ah,' he murmured, catching sight of Casey Junior puffing along the track, 'that must be it!' Replacing the map inside his pocket, he said, 'Well, little fellow, let's get goin'.' Holding the bundle securely in his beak he dived towards the train. Landing neatly on the roof of one of the cars he began to walk quickly along the top. 'Mrs Jumbo! . . . Oh, Mrs Jumbo!' he called as he went.

He passed from one car to another peering inside and calling all the time, 'Mrs Jumbo . . . calling Mrs Jumbo!'

A magnificent lion roared angrily at him through a ventilator and he drew back in haste. 'Oh . . . I . . . I beg your pardon. Huh, huh!' Tipping his hat he hurried on

Stopping over another ventilator he fanned himself. 'Mrs Jumboooooooo . . .!' he cried. 'Oh, where *is* that Mrs Jumbo?'

'Yoo hoo . . . yoo hoo . . .' The stork looked around, then jumped hastily to his feet. At the very front of the train elephant trunks were sticking out of a ventilator, wiggling and motioning the stork in their direction. 'This way, boy!' cried one elephant.

'In here! In here!' cried another. 'Yoo hoo! This is the place.'

The trunks disappeared inside the ventilator and the stork straddled the opening, peering down inside. Four elephants all gazed inquisitively at their visitor.

17

'Hey ... which one of
you ladies is expect-
ing?' The stork push-
ed his postman's cap
to the back of his head.

A well-rounded elephant named Catty drew
in her tummy and said, 'Not me!'

Miss Prissy looked annoyed. 'The very
idea!' she trumpeted.

Matriarch, who considered herself a very
important personage, snorted, 'Certainly not!'
Raising her long trunk she looked down its
length, then said in her snootiest voice, 'Over
there, of course!' She allowed the faintest of
smiles to crease her face as she indicated Mrs
Jumbo.

Mrs Jumbo lowered her head shyly, then looked directly at the stork, fluttering her eyes. Her trunk was wrapped bashfully around one leg and her heart was beating very fast. Clever Mr Stork had found her after all. All the smoke from Casey Junior had not fooled the wise bird. The stork hopped through the ventilator bars, tipped his hat and placed the little round bundle at her feet. From the brim of his cap he produced a book, then he felt in his vest pocket for his stubby pencil. Opening the book he commenced to read:

Here is a baby with eyes of blue,
Straight from heaven — right to you!

Mrs Jumbo's face was wreathed in smiles as she started to untie the wrappings. But the stork was not finished. 'Or if you prefer,' he said, 'you can have . . .' And he began to sing:

Straight from heaven up above,
Here is a baby for you to love!

The stork heaved a sigh of relief . . . his duty was almost done. Thrusting the book beneath Mrs Jumbo's nose he said, 'Sign here, please!' She read the printed words 'Received — one elephant', and, taking the pencil in her trunk, marked the book with an X. The stork replaced the book inside his vest pocket. 'Huh! Yeah! Well . . . oh, Mrs Jumbo . . . one moment, please!' Sweeping his peaked cap from his head he felt inside its rim and brought out a pitch pipe. 'This is still a part of

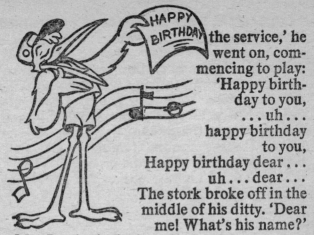

the service,' he went on, commencing to play: 'Happy birthday to you, ...uh... happy birthday to you, Happy birthday dear... uh...dear... The stork broke off in the middle of his ditty. 'Dear me! What's his name?'

Mrs Jumbo looked more shy than ever and batted her eyes. 'Junior,' she stammered.

'Oh . . . Jumbo Junior, huh!' The stork straightened up and cleared his throat. 'Mmmmm — Jumbo Junior . . . ahem!' Tooting a few notes on his pipe he bent over the round bundle to sing:

Happy birthday dear Jumbo Junior,
Happy birthday tooooooooooooooooo you!

As Mr Stork hit the final note he hopped up to the car ventilator and croaked, 'Goodbye, Mrs Jumbo . . . goodbye, Junior.' Then with a powerful swish of wings he disappeared from view.

Immediately the stork had departed, Mrs Jumbo gave her full attention to unwrapping her precious bundle. Four other female elephants sharing the compartment bent forward eagerly, for they too were very curious.

20

Giggles, an elephant who found humour in almost every situation remarked, 'I'm on pins and needles!'

Prissy replied, 'Isn't it thrilling?'

Giggles swayed her trunk. 'I'm all aflutter!'

Matriarch raised her tiny eyes heavenwards. She considered Giggles a stupid creature. 'Ah ...' she began, 'this is a proud, proud day!'

Catty, more impatient than the rest, cried out,' Well, hurry and open it, dearie!'

Giggles gave a small laugh. 'I'm just dying to see!'

Mrs Jumbo, quite unconcerned by her companion's remarks, took her time unwrapping the outer covering. At last her darling baby was revealed. He sat at his mother's feet with closed eyes, a cuddly, tiny grey elephant.

'Oooooooooooh!' chorused the four onlookers. 'Look at him! Just look at him!'

The baby stretched out his trunk, blinked, then rubbed his eyes.

'Oh, you sweet little thing! Oh ... ah! Isn't he cute?' said Giggles. 'Isn't he a darling little baby?'

Mrs Jumbo smiled proudly at her tiny offspring as the other elephants continued to heap praises upon his head.

Matriarch nodded. 'Adorable! I must agree. Simply adorable!'

Prissy stepped closer. 'Did you ever see anything so cunning?' The other elephants shook their heads.

'He's an utter darling.' said Giggles, who on occasion was very sweet-tempered.

'Kootchy, kootchy, kootchy, kootchy!' For once, Matriarch forgot her dignity and fussed

over the new arrival.

Suddenly, he wrinkled his trunk, raised his head in the air and sneezed violently. A pair of fantastically enormous ears flapped out on either side of him. For a moment there was a stunned silence. The rest of the elephants jerked back, utterly amazed by the huge, floppy ears. They could scarcely believe their eyes.

'Ohhhh! Ahhhhhhh!' they gasped in unison.

Matriarch looked down the length of her trunk. 'Is it possible?'

Prissy wrinkled her forehead. 'Isn't there some mistake?'

Catty drew a deep breath. There was nothing she loved more than a bit of scandal. 'Just look . . . just look at those — those — e-a-r-s.' She spelled out the word.

Giggles looked bewildered. 'Those what?' she asked foolishly. 'Oh . . .' and she raised her trunk knowingly. 'I get it! Those ears!' She burst into helpless laughter and leaning over the baby elephant, grabbed hold of one ear in her trunk. 'Aren't they funny? Uh ha,ha,ha,ha,ha,ha!'

Mrs Jumbo, puzzled at the first sight of her little son's colossal ears, felt outraged at the mockery from her companions. It was unjust . . . unfair! How could the baby help having the largest ears ever seen on an elephant? Angrily, she slapped Giggles with her trunk. Giggles squealed and jumped back, releasing the baby elephant's ear.

'Oh! Why! My goodness!' said Matriarch huffily.

'What a temper,' said Catty.

Protectively, Mrs Jumbo picked up her baby, placing him between her legs and glaring at the others.

'Gosh . . . what'd I do?' complained Giggles. 'Oh, tell me . . . did I say anything?'

'You made a perfectly harmless remark, my dear,' said Matriarch with a snort.

Giggles looked offended. 'I just said that they're funny ears — and they *are* funny!'

'They certainly are,' Catty smirked unkindly.

Prissy turned her head in the opposite direction to the new arrival. 'After all . . . who cares about her precious little Jumbo?'

'Jumbo!' sniffed Catty. 'You mean *Dumbo*!'

The four elephants burst into unkind laughter. 'Dumbo!' they exclaimed. 'That's good! That's very good!'

Mrs Jumbo scowled. She felt very angry with the other elephants. At that moment, little Dumbo looked up at his mother and grinned, love in his tiny bright eyes. Her heart melted. She would ignore the other elephant's unkind comments. Closing her ears to their mockery she slammed the partition separating her from her travelling companions. It closed with a heavy slam. She could still hear them commenting and saying, 'Oh . . . oh . . . oh!' With her heart full of love for her baby, she lay down beside Dumbo, wrapped him up in his ears and cuddled him. Soon, they were both asleep.

Night had fallen. Most of the animals aboard Casey Junior were sleeping as he tugged, steamed and puffed his way across the vast expanse of countryside. The train was climbing steadily, hedged in between mountain ranges clad in mysterious deep purple shadow. Tall pine trees on the lower ridges looked black in the half-light; overhead, the evening star blinked in a velvety sky and in deep gorges below, water cascaded into vast lakes.

A small passing wind caught the words of Casey Junior's song, carrying them along the tracks:

> I think I can...
> I think I can...
> I think I can...

The little train with its shiny red engine snorted and gasped as it climbed a steep gradient. Reaching the top of the hill, it heaved a great sigh, then chugged loudly down the other side. It snorted with relief as its wheels sang happily:

I thought I could . . .
I thought I could . . .
I thought I could . . .

When the tracks ran level again, Casey Junior gave a jubilant blast on its whistle, cutting the air like a knife. At a more leisurely pace, it continued on its winding way.

Another few hours passed into eternity, though the land was still bathed in the shadows of night. But now, the scenery was changing rapidly. Lights flickered on the outskirts of a still-sleeping town; buildings, shops and houses slid into view. Casey Junior decreased his speed for just ahead lay the railway station and the destination of the circus. With a sudden screech of brakes the train pulled up and the sleeping animals were jerked into wakefulness. In the elephant's quarters, Matriarch, Catty, Prissy and Giggles were slammed against a wall as several train cars bumped into each other.

'Whew! I shall complain,' said Matriarch in a tone of deep annoyance. 'That is not the best way to be woken up.'

'I quite agree,' answered Prissy, adjusting her little lemon cap which had slid over one eye and made her look like a pirate.

'Of all the nerve,' said Catty, brushing straw from her forelegs with her long grey trunk.

But Giggles was laughing and laughing. 'Wonder what happened to the little chap next door,' she giggled, referring to Dumbo. 'He probably took off . . . jet propelled.' She burst into further fits of laughter.

'Control yourself . . . do!' said Matriarch in her iciest tones. 'Here come the roustabouts.'

The circus attendants had been the first to jump down on to the station platform and now they opened up the elephant's compartment. The magnificent and powerful animals were very useful when there were wagons to push and tents to erect. As they walked down the ramp, Dumbo sniffed the chilly night air and looked up at the sky. He blinked, then looked up at his mother who was watching him fondly. He jumped as lightning flashed in the distant mountains but she nudged him gently, saying, 'There's no need to worry, son . . . I'm with you.' Within minutes, there was noise, bustle and commotion everywhere. Already inside the huge circus field, tents were being erected, animal cages rolled into position and sleeping quarters made ready.

The roustabouts, men who handled the heavy labour at each site, were glad to be at the end of yet another journey. They sang as they worked, tossing stakes to each other and pounding them vigorously into the soggy ground:

Hike! Uh . . . Hike! Uh . . .
Hike! Uh . . . Hike!
We work all day, we work all night,
We never learned to read or write,
We're happy-hearted roustabouts . . .

The men raised their voices in song as they worked. The circus field was flickering with a multitude of torches flashing in all directions. Mrs Jumbo and even tiny Dumbo pounded stakes into the ground. When that task was complete, the elephants formed a line and marched across the field. Dumbo was at the end with a lantern balanced on his curly tail. As he walked behind his mother, it swayed gently to and fro, causing the men to laugh.

The roustabouts continued singing:

> We don't know when we get our pay,
> But when we do, we throw it away,
> We get our pay when children say,
> With happy hearts, it's circus day ...
> TODAY!

The men paused for a moment to sort out giant rolls of canvas. Within a little while the elephants were helping to put up the Big Top. Dumbo watched his mother and wanted to join in but he was far too small. The roustabouts laughed good-naturedly at his attempts. Already, he was a firm favourite with them.

At last, tents flapped in the wind and the work was finished. The men called out to each other, joking and talking of the hot breakfast they expected, the rest they were looking forward to. The seemingly endless pounding was over — at least for another season. With a rousing cheer, they headed for the tent marked 'Refreshments.'

By the following morning, the rain had stopped and the sun peeped shyly from behind a sombre grey cloud. A band was marching from the circus grounds towards the street and the notes of the trombone, the tuba and the piccolo blended with the great bass drum. Astride a handsome chestnut horse, the ringmaster rode proudly into the street tipping his hat to the crowds which had gathered. It was evident that the circus was very popular and about to receive a royal welcome. Four zebras with elegantly striped coats pulled a lion cage through the street amidst 'Ooooohs' and

'Ahhhs' from the open-mouthed children. many of whom had never seen a circus before. Behind the lions came the tigers, then a gorilla standing up behind the bars of his cage and dramatically beating his chest. He pulled violently at the bars. Suddenly, one of them came away in his hand and he looked very surprised. To the delight and amusement of the crowds, he replaced it. The children rocked with laughter.

Even Mrs Hippo pulled a wagon after her and bad-tempered camels, lavishly bedecked with red and gold trimmings, snapped and yawned as men rode on their humped backs.

The clowns came next . . . and they were a special favourite with children and adults alike. They cavorted, turned somersaults, played instruments, threw custard pies at each other and blew up balloons which were released among the happy children, making them laugh and jump for joy.

The elephants came last of all. They looked magnificent, beautifully dressed in silk caps trimmed with gold braid with richly embroidered cloths of blue and silver on their backs. Tucked behind their ears were bunches of blossom to announce the welcome return of spring. Little Dumbo was at the very end of the line, a tiny doll sitting erect on his back. The children clapped their hands with glee. Immediately, they all fell in love with the cute baby elephant and took him to their hearts.

When the circus had paraded through the centre of town, Mrs Jumbo and Dumbo returned to their quarters. It was time for Dumbo to have a bath. He loved the idea of

sitting in a tub of soapy water filled with hundreds of tiny coloured bubbles. He lost no time in playing games and sitting back, kicked, splashed, swished his trunk and blew bubbles at his mother. It was all great fun though Mrs Jumbo was more concerned with washing his ears. It was a difficult task, partly because of their enormous size and partly because he would not sit still. At last, Mrs Jumbo had washed her baby all over. She doused him with fresh water then lifted him from the tub and sat him on the floor. Jumping immediately to his feet, he shook his head vigorously to remove water from his ears. Then he began to play more games. Kicking his feet in the air, he trumpeted as loudly as a tiny elephant could, and then, grinning at his mother, scooted behind her feet to try and hide.

Mrs Jumbo pretended not to see him and Dumbo thought it was great fun. Running round and round his mother's legs, he grabbed her tail and peeked at her. She pretended to chase him and little Dumbo raced across the floor, but suddenly tripped over his big ears and fell flat on his face.

Mrs Jumbo's smile turned to an expression of concern. Only now was she realising what a problem her little son's huge ears might be. But Dumbo wasn't worried. Smiling, he clambered to his feet. Mrs Jumbo's face softened with love and she patted her brave little baby on the head, nuzzling him lovingly with her trunk. Little Dumbo gazed up at her with adoration in his bright eyes and twined his trunk around hers.

Later that day, people began to pour into
the circus grounds. It was almost time for the
show to begin. Crowds flocked towards the
Big Top eager to fill the seats as the ticket-
sellers called out, 'Step right up and get your
tickets! Hurry, hurry, now!' They moved
amongst the milling crowds. 'Get your
tickets,' they cried. 'Tickets for the side shows
before you go into the Big Top!'

Close to the main circus tent, Dumbo stood
with his mother. A group of rowdy boys hung
over the ropes separating the public from the
animals. Dumbo approached them shyly,
flapping his ears and trumpeting.

One of the boys, a skinny youth with a dirty face and clothes to match guffawed rudely. 'Hey, look! Ain't that the funniest thing you ever saw? Look . . . look at his ears!' He pointed mockingly at Dumbo. The little elephant didn't understand and wiggled his ears again.

'Hey, guys . . . look at me.' Stripping off his grubby topcoat, the nasty boy flapped it behind his head and made faces. 'Skinny's an elephant . . . Skinny's an elephant . . .' The other boys laughed loudly and Mrs Jumbo, blinking back tears, looked very hurt. She couldn't bear to see her dear baby made into an object of ridicule.

Protectively, she reached forward, picking Dumbo up in her powerful trunk. Defiantly, she turned her back on the nasty, jeering boys. 'Yah . . . boo!' shouted the skinny youth. 'You can't hide him from us.'

'Yeah!' chimed in one of the others. 'His ears are still stickin' out!'

'Come on . . . we wanna see him,' called another grimy-faced urchin. 'We wanna laugh. That's what we came for!' Leaning forward, he pulled hard on little Dumbo's tail.

Dumbo, frightened now, ran for protection behind his mother's front legs. Another hand tried to pull him forward and grabbed the baby elephant's right ear. Holding it aloft the boy yelled, 'Hey! Look . . . the biggest sling-shot in the world!'

Alarmed and angry, Mrs Jumbo spanked the horrid boy with her trunk as he tried to slip beneath the ropes. 'Hey! Cut that out! You're hurting me. Help! Murder!' he squealed.

Unfortunately, his screeches attracted the attention of several people. The ringmaster dashed forward. 'Now . . . now . . . what's going on?' he yelled.

Mrs Jumbo waved her trunk angrily, picked up a bale of hay and tossed it in the air. The ringmaster thrashed his whip. 'Down, Mrs Jumbo! Down!' he shouted. Frightened by the crowds who were closing in, and by the crack of the whip, Mrs Jumbo seized a bucket in her trunk and flung that after the hay, a wild expression on her face. The ringmaster's whip caught the side of her cheek and she reared up. 'Surround her,' shouted the ringmaster.

'Tie her down.'

Little Dumbo, frightened and distressed at the unhappy events taking place, whimpered and ran towards his mother. An attendant pulled him away. Mrs Jumbo fought with the men who were struggling to put her in chains. She managed to break away and trumpeting loudly, knocked over a pole, breaking it in two. 'Down! Calm down . . . calm down!' the irate ringmaster yelled and cracked his whip more angrily than before. His actions did not help the situation.

Panic-stricken and worried about her baby, noble Mrs Jumbo picked up the ringmaster by his leg, and dropped him head first into a tub of water. The circus folk tried not to laugh for when he rose to the surface he was red with anger and his shirt front popped upwards, hitting him on the nose. But it did nothing to improve his temper. 'Lock her up,' he commanded. 'Do it at once. She's mad . . . quite mad!' Shaking water from his hair he strode furiously to his tent to change into dry clothes.

Poor Mrs Jumbo was overpowered by sheer force of numbers and within a short space of time was locked inside a wagon. Huge notices on the outside read: 'Danger. Mad Elephant. Keep Off!'

She stood in a far corner, grief-stricken. Alone and misunderstood, she wept bitterly, not for herself, but for dear little Dumbo. Without her protection, what would become of him?

Inside the elephant's tent, Matriarch, Catty, Prissy and Giggles were indulging in their favourite pastime — gossip! There was nothing they loved better and dear Mrs Jumbo's unfortunate fall from grace had provided some choice tidbits. The four female elephants stood together in a group, nodding and shaking their heads. Little Dumbo sat alone, some distance away. He felt unwanted, an outcast in the community, and as he looked at the tub marked 'Mrs Jumbo' where his mother had recently frolicked with him, giant tears rolled down his cheeks.

While Dumbo wept, Giggles laughed. 'It was so funny,' she was saying. 'Oh, my dear, can you bear it? When she doused the ringmaster, I just thought I'd die!'

'Well, personally,' said Prissy with a toss of her head, 'I think she went a bit too far!'

Matriarch took up the conversation. 'After all,' she said in superior tones, 'one mustn't forget that one is a lady!'

'Oh . . . of course, you're right, dear . . . you're right as usual,' responded Giggles.

Prissy swished her trunk and raised it to her mouth, trying to look angelic. 'Oh, well . . . I suppose that's mother love.'

'But it's certainly no excuse for what she did,' contributed Giggles and unable to control herself, she went off into fits of explosive laughter again.

'Mother love covers a multitude of sins!' Prissy looked thoughtful. 'And Mrs Jumbo . . . she used to have such a sweet disposition.' She shook her head regretfully. 'I don't know what things are coming to!'

Dumbo could not help overhearing the conversation and it only served to make him sadder than ever. And it was all because he had these enormous ears . . . if only . . . if only . . . but what *could* he do?

In the far corner of the tent lay an overturned sack of peanuts. If the elephants had not been so busy gossiping, they might have noticed a mouse's tail sticking out from the sack.

However, they were far too interested in the latest scandal. The peanuts scattered as a cheeky chocolate-brown mouse emerged, carrying a peanut in his arms. Turning, he looked across at the group of elephants. 'Hmmmmm . . .' he said with a tiny mouse snort. 'Gossiping — as usual! A guy can't eat in peace!' Hopping on to one peanut, he began to open up another one, shaking his head in disgust. 'Dear, dear, dear . . . haven't they anything better to do?' he asked of no one in particular. Flipping a peanut in the air, he caught it in his mouth.

'Girls . . . girls . . . just listen. Have I got a trunkful of dirt!' Catty smirked, pleased with the immediate reaction to her remark.

'Well, go on darling . . . go on . . . don't keep us in suspense,' urged the others.

Catty lifted the edge of Prissy's ear and said in a stage whisper, 'Well . . . I heard today that they've put her in solitary confinement. Yes, Mrs Jumbo is completely shut away!'

'No!' Matriarch sounded genuinely shocked.

'You don't mean it?' chorused the other elephants.

'I do!' Catty nodded her head emphatically, a look of smug satisfaction on her face.

'Oh! Oh! How awful for her!' Prissy looked thoughtful. 'I must admit to feeling sorry. I can't say I blame *her* for anything!'

'You're absolutely right. It's all the fault of that . . . that . . . f-r-e-a-k.' Spelling out the word, she stole a swift glance in Dumbo's direction. He was still seated beside his mother's wash-tub, crying bitterly. But pity

did not stir her soul for the little, lonely creature. Catty was not the pitying type. Prissy snorted her contempt. 'Yes ... him with those extraordinary ears that only a mother could love!' All the elephants went off into wild peals of laughter but the little mouse whose name was Tim, looked up indignantly.

Glancing at Dumbo he said aloud, 'What's the matter wid his ears? I don't see nothin' wrong with 'em!' He shook his head. 'I think they're cute!' He munched another peanut. Neither the grieving Dumbo or the gossipy elephants were aware of little Tim's presence so he continued to eat, and to listen, undisturbed.

Matriarch composed herself then looked sternly at her companions. 'Ladies . . . ladies . . .' she trumpeted. 'It's no laughing matter at all!'

'Oh . . . she's right, girls,' agreed Giggles, still trying desperately to stifle her laughter.

Matriarch looked haughtily round the tent.

'Don't forget that we elephants have always walked with dignity!' She pointed her trunk in Dumbo's direction. '*His* disgrace is our shame!' Poor little Dumbo wanted the floor to open and swallow him up — why did everybody have to be so unkind?

'Yes, Matriarch, what you say is true!' Prissy always agreed with Matriarch, for secretly she was a little afraid of her.

Giggles nodded her head. 'Oh . . . indeed it is . . . yes!'

Catty raised her eyes towards the tent ceiling. 'Frankly, I wouldn't eat at the same bale of hay with him!' She grinned cruelly.

'Nor I . . . Nor I . . . Me neither, dearie,' echoed the other elephants.

Dumbo, tears blinding his eyes, rose unsteadily to his feet and walked towards the gossiping group. All he wanted was a kind word, he felt so alone.

'Oh dear . . . uh . . . here he comes now!' whispered Catty.

Matriarch looked annoyed. 'Humph! Pretend you don't see him! Shhhhhhhh!' Deliberately, she looked in the opposite direction. Following her cue, all the elephants turned their backs on tiny Dumbo.

Tim the mouse, who was still balanced on a pile of peanuts, ceased munching. 'How do you like that?' he asked. 'Givin' him the cold shoulder!'

Dumbo, snubbed by the unfriendly elephants, walked dejectedly towards the tent exit. Tim watched him sorrowfully. 'Poor little guy! There he goes . . . without a friend in the world!' Tim lowered his chin onto his fist. 'Nobody to turn to!' Suddenly, the mouse jumped to his feet, tossing aside his peanut. Doubling up his fists, he swung them determinedly. 'Ho! I'll do somethin' about this!' With a show of resolution, he strutted along the ground.

The elephants were in a huddle when he reached them. For all their bulk, Tim knew their weakness.

Deliberately, he moved in amongst them. Catty spotted him first. She emitted a shrill cry of alarm. 'Look . . . a mouse . . . a mouse!'

There was immediate panic. Two of the elephants in an attempt to get away, ran head first into each other. The other two squealed in alarm. Tim took full advantage of the moment. Climbing on to the branch of a tree, he waved his tiny hands in the air, stuck out his tongue and made faces at the scared beasts. 'So you like to pick on little guys, huh?' he yelled. 'Well, why don't you pick on me?'

'Oh . . . oh dear!' gasped Matriarch, ducking behind some canvas.

'Oh . . . oh . . . oh!' shrieked Giggles, trying to climb a pole.

Catty clutched at a rope and all the time, Tim continued to bait them. He placed his hands on his hips, looking disgusted at their absurd behaviour. 'A proud race,' he snorted. 'Hmmmm . . . overstuffed hay bags!' Whistling, he walked all round them adopting a bold, Napoleonic pose. 'Boo!' he shouted. 'Still afraid of a mouse . . . ho,ho . . . boy! Wait till I tell the little guy!'

Tim looked round the tent is sudden bewilderment. 'Now . . . where's he got to? Where is he?'

There wasn't a sign of Dumbo but then Tim noticed a small trunk sticking out of a hay pile. 'Dumbo,' called Tim, 'you can come out now!' The trunk disappeared inside the hay. Tim looked surprised. 'Hmmmmm . . . golly! Maybe I scared him, too!'

Stretching out his hands towards the hay, Tim called, 'Look, Dumbo, I'm your *friend!* Come on out, won't cha? Aw . . . come on . . . you're not really afraid of little me, are ya?' He looked appealingly at the hay pile.

There was not a movement. Tim's shoulders sagged. 'Ya there?' he cried. He spread his hands helplessly. 'Musta overdid it in there — don't know my own strength sometimes!' An idea struck him. With a grin he swept his cap from his head, revealing a peanut inside. Flipping the peanut in the air he caught it and replaced his cap on his head.

'Dumbo,' he called coaxingly. 'Look what I got for ya!' Dumbo's trunk poked through the hay and cautiously sniffed the peanut. Little

Tim moved backwards. 'Ah . . . ah . . . ah . . . you gotta come out foist!' The trunk made a slight movement and the peanut was sucked right out of Tim's hand. He looked in surprise at the empty shell as it floated towards the ground.

'Too bad you don't trust me,' said the mouse. He strolled away from the hay yet made sure that his voice carried to Dumbo. 'Too bad . . . because I thought . . . uh . . . well . . . you and me . . . we might get your mother outta the clink!'

Tim was aware of a faint movement in the hay and then Dumbo peeked out. Tim pretended not to notice him. 'But I guess you wouldn't be interested,' he continued. 'So long, Dumbo.' Putting his hands in his pockets he whistled in a carefree way. But in the next instant, he was raised high off the ground. Little Dumbo had emerged and picked Tim up in his trunk. The tiny mouse and Dumbo grinned at each other. There was an immediate understanding — they were going to be friends.

Gently, Dumbo lowered Tim to the ground. 'Well, that's more like it.' He surveyed Dumbo. 'Ya know, your ma ain't crazy!'

Dumbo nodded in agreement and lay down and Tim leaned against his trunk. 'She's just broken-hearted!' went on Tim. 'It ain't nobody's fault you got them big ears!' He stuffed his hands in his pockets.

At the mention of ears, Dumbo looked distressed and flapped them completely over his face. Tim scratched his chin. 'Oh, oh boy . . . I sure stepped in it that time! Aw gee,

Dumbo, I think your ears are beautiful.' Tim climbed in between Dumbo's ears. 'Sure . . . as a matter of fact, I think they're very decorative!' Encouraged, Dumbo wiggled one of them. 'Ya know,' said Tim, 'lots of people with big ears are famous!'

Dumbo shyly showed his face, blinking happily. It was so wonderful to hear kind words instead of ridicule and abuse. He looked with gratitude at his tiny friend.

Tim rubbed his nose thoughtfully. 'Ho, ho . . . boy! All we gotta do is build an act! Yeah, make you a star! A headliner!' Tim ran down the length of Dumbo's trunk. 'Dumbo the great! Oh . . . but the great what?' Tim jumped from the end of Dumbo's trunk. Thoughtfully, he began to pace the floor. Dumbo got up too, and taking Tim's tail in his trunk, paced with him. 'Ya know, Dumbo . . . we gotta get an idea . . . not just any idea . . . somethin' colossal like uh . . .' Tim suddenly stopped talking. In the circus tent nearby he could see the ringmaster engaged in conversation with one of his assistants. In a loud voice, the ringmaster said, 'Have I got an idea! And what an idea!'

Tim pricked up his ears, but said, 'Huh, that ringmaster never had an idea in his life!'

The ringmaster went on talking to his flunky. 'Just visualise . . . one elephant climbs on the back of another elephant until, finally, all seventeen elephants have constructed an enormous pyramid of pachyderms.'

The flunky's eyes rolled and he dropped his pitch fork. 'Yes.' continued the ringmaster. 'I step out . . . I blow the whistle! The trumpets are trumpeting . . .'

Tim strained his ears, listening with interest. 'And now,' said the ringmaster dramatically, 'now comes the grand finale!'

'Yeah,' muttered the flunky interestedly, 'but what *is* the grand finale?'

The ringmaster rubbed his chin doubtfully. 'Humph! Darned if I know.'

Tim looked disgusted. 'As I suspected, that one never knew nothin'.'

The ringmaster shrugged. 'Well . . . maybe it'll come to me in a vision while I dream. I'm off to bed. Goodnight, Joe.'

'Goodnight, boss,' replied the flunky, retrieving the pitchfork he had dropped.

The two men moved out of earshot. Tim glanced at Dumbo, his expression thoughtful. 'A grand finale,' he murmured. Suddenly he jumped high in the air. 'A grand finale! Dumbo . . . I've got it! *You* are the grand finale!'

Dumbo shook his head. He didn't understand his little friend at all. How could *he* be the grand finale? But Tim was too excited to explain at the moment. Waving his hat in the air he cried, 'I'll be back in a minute, Dumbo. I'm gonna take care of your future!' In the twinkling of an eye, he had vanished.

Tim, the sharp little mouse, with his hat at a rakish angle, scurried swiftly from Dumbo's tent and made his way into the circus grounds. It was late and there were very few of the circus folk about. Mostly they were in bed, for the first few days after settling into new quarters were very exhausting.

Tim sniffed the air. It was a fine, mild night and moths and fireflies danced in the faint breeze and the sky was twinkling with stars. But Tim paid little attention to the delights of spring. His mind was fully occupied with thoughts of how to make Dumbo famous. The poor little fellow deserved a break.

Tim peered cautiously about him then dashed behind a thick rope, his tail sticking up as he ran. When he reached the ringmaster's tent, he paused. Stealthily lifting a flap, he peered beneath it. Tim nodded his head with satisfaction. From inside the tent came deep, regular snores. The situation couldn't be better. Swiftly and silently, Tim scurried inside.

The ringmaster lay snoring on his bed, his hat still perched on his head. Beside the bed was a trunk and Tim climbed up its side and stared at a bunch of keys and an open watch lying on the trunk's surface. Tim struck the watch with the bunch of keys and they made a loud 'tinging' sound. Tim drew close to the sleeping ringmaster's ear. 'I am the voice of your subconscious mind, your inspiration!' he hissed. 'Now . . . concentrate. Remember . . . remember your pyramid of elephants standing in the ring waiting for the grand finale!'

The ringmaster stirred uneasily, muttering as he slept, 'The grand finale!'

Dramatically, Tim whispered, 'You are seeing that grand finale now!'

Again, the ringmaster tossed and turned. 'The grand finale,' he said distinctly.

Cheekily, Tim leaned closer. 'How's the reception? Comin' through OK?' The ringmaster mumbled.

Tim straightened up. 'Good!' He squared his shoulders. 'Suddenly, from the sidelines comes your grand finale. Gallopin' across the arena! He jumps from a springboard to a platform at the very pinnacle of your pyramid!' Tim paused and hopped on to the ringmaster's hat and hung from its brim. Taking a deep breath he continued, 'He waves the flag for a glorious finish!'

'Finish!' muttered the ringmaster, still snoring but certainly getting Tim's hypnotic message.

'And who *is* your grande finale?' shouted Tim. 'The little elephant with the big ears! The world's mightiest midget! Dumbo . . .

Dumbo!' Now that Tim had planted the idea in the ringmaster's mind he dashed away to a hiding place inside the tent to observe what would happen next. The ringmaster snorted in his sleep, then kept repeating, 'Dumbo . . . Dumbo . . . Dumbo . . .' The mouse smiled — a wide smile of satisfaction. It looked as if his clever plan was going to work. Presently, the ringmaster moved, opened his eyes, sat up with a smile on his ruddy face and yelled, 'I got it . . . I got it . . . the BIG idea!'

The very next day the ringmaster was ready to put what he felt was his own brilliant idea into operation. A large audience sat in the main circus tent, bubbling with excitement. Children watched wide-eyed as the ringmaster strode importantly into the centre of the ring. Elephants clustered all around him, the spotlight focusing on the exciting scene.

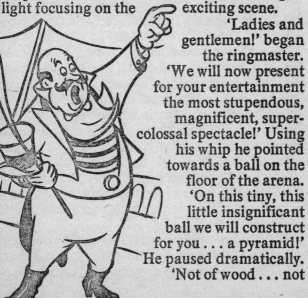

'Ladies and gentlemen!' began the ringmaster. 'We will now present for your entertainment the most stupendous, magnificent, super-colossal spectacle!' Using his whip he pointed towards a ball on the floor of the arena. 'On this tiny, this little insignificant ball we will construct for you . . . a pyramid!' He paused dramatically. 'Not of wood . . . not of stone ... not of steel ...'

Catty the elephant leaned over and whispered in Matriarch's ear, 'To hear him talk, you'd think he was going to do it!'

'The stuffed shirt!' snorted Matriarch, as the ringmaster continued his pompous speech.

'Yes ... a living, breathing pyramid of ponderous, pulsating, pulchritudinous pachyderms.' The ringmaster threw his arms in the air in what he hoped was a regal gesture, but unfortunately his shirt front rolled up, hitting him beneath the chin. Angrily, he thrust it down and shouted 'I give you ... the elephants!'

Puffed up with his own importance, the ringmaster blew a whistle and cracked his whip. The elephants marched round in a circle. Matriarch drew level with the ball and proudly raising her head, placed her front feet upon it. Prissy came next and the two elephants entwined their trunks as Matriarch helped Prissy to clamber on her back. Prissy was not concentrating, for she was too busy seeking applause from the audience. She slipped, sitting on Matriarch's head.

Matriarch scowled crossly. 'Aren't we a bit clumsy?' she asked in acid tones.

Prissy hastily stood up balancing herself carefully. She did not wish to upset Matriarch.

Catty came next and Prissy groaned. 'Gaining a little weight, aren't you honey?' she asked sarcastically.

'You're no cream puff yourself, dearie,' came the rude reply.

'Quiet up there!' snapped Matriarch who

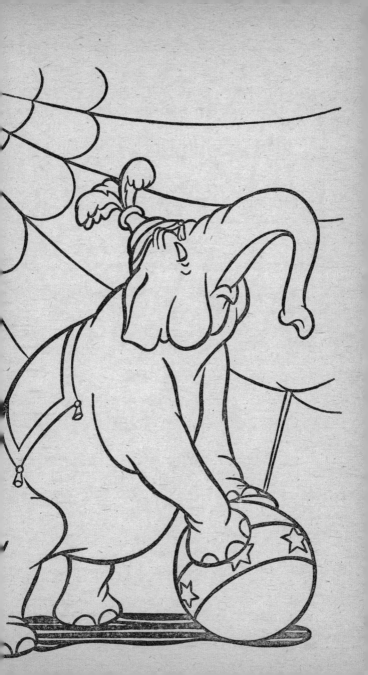

was bearing the full brunt of the ringmaster's idea of a pyramid. 'Attend to your work, girls. And Prissy . . . take your foot out of my eye. You clumsy ox!'

The entire pyramid began to sway. 'Steady, girls,' Matriarch said in a worried undertone. She didn't want a whole pyramid of elephants crashing down on her head.

'Oh . . . ohhhhhhh!' gasped the audience, holding their breaths in awe.

One elephant did fall through the air but was caught on the end of Prissy's trunk and she managed to haul herself up again. Tim the mouse, was watching from behind the curtains. 'Boy! That was a close one!' he

sighed mopping his forehead. 'They're almost ready now, Dumbo. 'He turned to face his friend who was waiting his cue to enter the circus tent. 'Don't forget to wave that flag!'

Dumbo raised the flag in his trunk, waving it in the air. 'OK ... OK ...' said Tim. 'Don't wave it no more. Nor right now. I saw ya.' Dumbo stopped waving the flag and listened to what Tim was saying. 'Now look ... all you gotta do is run out, see! Jump on the spring-board. All right?' Dumbo nodded.

'Right!' said Tim. 'Now show me just how you gonna do it!'

Dumbo drew back and took aim as if jumping onto the springboard. He made a

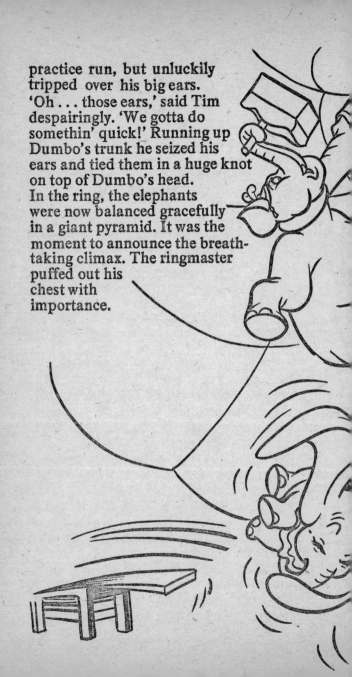

practice run, but unluckily
tripped over his big ears.
'Oh . . . those ears,' said Tim
despairingly. 'We gotta do
somethin' quick!' Running up
Dumbo's trunk he seized his
ears and tied them in a huge knot
on top of Dumbo's head.
In the ring, the elephants
were now balanced gracefully
in a giant pyramid. It was the
moment to announce the breath-
taking climax. The ringmaster
puffed out his
chest with
importance.

'Ladies and gentlemen, you have seen the impossible accomplished in front of your faces. Seven jungle giants — each one weighing —'

Matriarch glared at the ringmaster. 'Pompous windbag! Why doesn't he come to the point?' she snapped.

'Each one weighing,' continued the ringmaster, 'not one ounce less than forty-five hundred pounds. And now I present the world's smallest elephant who will spring from this springboard,' and he pointed up to it, 'in one mighty leap to the very top of this pyramid waving his little flag for the grand finale! Ladies and gentlemen . . . I give you . . . DUMBO!'

Dumbo jumped with fright when he heard his name. 'Go on,' said Tim, 'get goin'!' But Dumbo suddenly had stage-fright and remained rooted to the spot. 'What's the matter with ya? Dumbo! That's your cue. You're on, Dumbo!'

Tim's urgent prompting didn't help one bit. This was no time to be fussy. Action was needed — and fast! Producing a long pin, Tim stuck it in Dumbo's rump. The little elephant took off at top speed, leapt in the air and bounced on to the springboard. The audience watched with bated breath. But the fast flight through the air had loosened the knot in Dumbo's ears. It untied and as Dumbo raced along the springboard, he tripped. A great gasp rose from the people below. As he fell, Dumbo's weight caused the springboard to jerk violently and in the next second, he was hurtling through the air at an alarming speed.

He missed the pyramid and sailed right over the top of it.

With a crash, he landed at Matriarch's feet. Startled, she was thrown off-balance and wobbled precariously. Desperately, she attempted to support the elephants above her. But it was no use ... one after the other, those at the top came crashing down. Panic stricken, people jumped to their feet and started screaming. During the turbulence which followed, little Dumbo sat at the edge of the ring, shattered by his experience. His eyes were closed, his long ears flopped on the ground and his brave little flag still flapped.in his trunk.

Tim, peeking from behind the curtains, was aghast at the pandemonium and clapped his hands over his eyes. He couldn't bear to look. 'What a mess ... what a mess ...' he groaned aloud.

Vainly, the ringmaster sought to bring the situation to order but it was hopeless. He shuddered, cast a wild look round the ring, dropped his whip — and fainted!

Matriarch, who prided herself on keeping her head in an emergency, struggled to maintain some sort of balance. Several elephants on the lower part of the pyramid were still balancing on her back. The ball on which she was standing started to roll away. Matriarch attempted to move with it, swaying perilously. Dumbo finally opened his eyes, blinking rapidly. Alarmed by the noise and confusion he jumped to his feet and tore round and round the ring. Matriarch caught up with him tapping him smartly on the back.

At that precise moment, Dumbo was certainly *not* in her good books. Terrified of the angry look in her eye, Dumbo rushed on but tripped over his ears, turning a complete somersault. Unable to pull herself back in time, Matriarch fell over him. That was the final disruption. The pyramid disintegrated completely.

One elephant in an effort to save herself grabbed a trapeze, pulling it down on top of her. Another flew through the air, landing on a bicycle. A trouper to the end, she tried to ride it but fell off with a resounding thud. Several other animals stampeded a platform inside the ring and with their combined weight, it caved in. Giggles bounced into a safety net — and broke it! Catty and Prissy, seeking a channel of escape charged into a pole. It snapped — then the circus tent collapsed.

The scene was a shambles. When the last of the people had fled, when the dust had finally settled, Dumbo's tiny trunk could be seen sticking up through a hole in the green canvas. His brave little flag was still waving in the breeze. Seconds later, that too broke and the flag fluttered to the ground.

Dumbo's mighty leap — and his fast fall from grace — had brought the ringmaster to a swift decision. The circus would move on at once. As for Dumbo, new plans would have to be made for his future, an entirely different type of act. Never again would he be allowed to create such havoc. The ringmaster, a pompous man by nature, felt degraded by recent events. The fact that he had fainted in front of his audience had been a humiliating experience, too.

After a night of pacing back and forth, twirling his long, waxed moustache and watching his flunkies clear away the debris, he thought he had come up with an idea for Dumbo's future; but for the moment he kept it to himself.

By the following evening, the huge field recently occupied by the circus was empty and Casey Junior, the valiant, puffing train was loaded, ready to start yet another journey. Although the weather was mild, a light misty rain was falling and the roustabouts were happy to see the last of the animals safely into

3

their compartments.

From the elephant's section came a low buzz of conversation. Catty, Giggles, Matriarch and Prissy were engaged in an exchange of gossip. None of them had emerged unscathed from the fracas, and at the moment were only too ready to air their views — and their indignation. Matriarch groaned as the train swayed. Her trunk was in a sling and she felt very undignified. 'Oh,' she exploded, 'I never thought I'd live to see the Big Top fall!'

Prissy limped painfully forward, a crutch attached to her right leg. 'Because of that . . . that Dumbo . . . I can never show my face in that town again!'

Giggles nodded agreement. Even a nod was a painful process. A water bag was tied around her head and she sported a magnificent black eye. Her tail of which she had always been justifiably proud was bandaged in a splint. 'Just look . . . look at my beautiful

tail,' she groaned. Today, she was not in a mood to laugh and giggle.

Matriarch looked very angry. 'I'd just like to spank the daylights out of him!' To add emphasis to her words she swung her trunk from its sling. 'Ohhhhhh, ohhhhhh!' she moaned and hastily replaced it.

Catty, who had been silent for a while looked smug and self-satisfied. Stepping forward she adjusted the ice bag balanced on her aching head. 'Spank him? That won't be necessary, dearie! They fixed him good!'

'What do you mean?' Matriarch sniffed.

'What did they do? Did they beat him?' enquired Giggles, whose look implied that she hoped they had.

'What is it, darling. Do tell us!' coaxed Prissy.

'Come, come, now!' Matriarch adopted her self-righteous tone. 'I demand to know!'

'Very well!' Catty could not hold out any longer. 'Well . . . they've gone and made him . . . oh dear, I just can't say it!' She hung her head, looking ashamed.

'Out with it!' said Matriarch impatiently.

Catty jerked her head upward and stared straight ahead. 'They've made him . . . a *clown*!' She stumbled over the word.

The other elephants drew back in shocked amazements. 'A clown?' they queried.

'No!' said Giggles. 'Oh, no!'

'Yes,' said Catty. 'I have it on good authority.'

'Oh . . . the *shame* of it.' Matriarch was outraged. 'An elephant acting as a clown! Let us take a solemn vow! From now on he —

Dumbo — is no longer an elephant!'

Solemnly, the other elephants put their trunks together in a vow of approval.

Casey Junior puffed, tugged and steamed his way across the countryside and quite soon had reached the new circus site. By the following night, everything was spick and span and the crowds were ready to be welcomed. Little Dumbo had been briefed by the ringmaster about his new act and though he found it very bewildering, there was little he could do except obey.

The circus tent was packed to capacity, the lions and tigers had been into the ring and received terrific applause. Now it was time for Dumbo to go into the ring. This time he couldn't afford to make mistakes. He drew a deep, quivering breath.

The circus clowns were a great favourite

with the children and Dumbo's performance would serve to enhance their popularity. Dressed as a baby, a rattle clutched in his trunk, he stepped warily on to a platform. The platform was raised to the top of a tall building erected in the ring's centre with an illusion of fire and flames engulfing it. From the great height of the platform, Dumbo gazed at the audience far below. Patiently he waited, watching the flames mount even higher.

Below in the circus ring, a clown was dressed as a woman. He wore an elephant's head mask and dashed frantically back and forth waving his arms, pretending to be Dumbo's mother. 'Help! Mr. Fireman . . . save my poor baby! Help! Ohhh . . . save my child!' He pointed upwards at Dumbo.

The children called out, 'Oooohhh . . . ahhhhh!' as fire trucks arrived, carrying clowns dressed in firemen's uniforms. Jumping from their truck they rushed across the ring, placing a ladder against the burning building. Turning with a wide grin to the audience, one of the clowns rapidly climbed the ladder but halfway up, lost his footing and slid to the bottom once more, falling flat on his stomach. The audience roared their appreciation.

Another truck arrived, its ladder cranked into mid-air with clowns dressed as firemen perched upon it. As it was hoisted close to the top of the building, all the clowns fell off. Another clown dashed into the ring dragging a hose with a fire hydrant attached and filling a water pistol, he squirted water into a nearby

clown's face. Children shrieked their approval and clapped their hands.

Dumbo, feeling very isolated on the top of the building, blinked unhappily at the scene taking place below. He knew the fire wasn't real — he knew he wouldn't be burned — but he felt very miserable in his new role as baby clown. Everyone else was having a good time. The clowns continued their funny antics, throwing buckets of water over each other, watering tiny blossoms in flower boxes and watching them expand rapidly into enormous blooms, generally having fun as they played their tricks on each other. Their jesting was richly appreciated; the crowds lapped it up.

Dumbo blinked pathetically. A clown mounted the ladder and when he reached the top he produced a giant-sized fan, vigorously fanning the baby elephant. Children were enchanted. A fireman took a hot-dog from his pocket and roasted it over the flames which were mounting higher and higher. Feeling nervous, Dumbo drew back.

The clown in the elephant's mask began to yell again, 'Save my baby!'

Four firemen held out a net at the base of the building. Clowns shouted up to Dumbo, 'Come on . . . jump! We'll save ya!'

Dumbo looked uncertainly at the net. It was a long way down. 'Hurry up! Hurry up!' they continued to yell. 'We'll save ya! Come on, jump! Come on!'

Dumbo leaned forward, his rattle still clutched in his trunk. Below, the audience waited, breathless with anticipation. To Dumbo they were a sea of white faces . . . a confused blur. Even as the clowns and children in the audience were urging him to jump, a clown clambered up the back of the building, picked up a board and swung it at Dumbo. It hit him and in the next instant he was off the platform and hurtling through the air. He still clutched his rattle and his ears flapped as he descended ... head first into the net ... then right into a bucket of plaster hidden beneath it. Struggling to regain his breath, Dumbo sat up in the tub, white plaster streaming down his face. The exciting performance had brought the audience to their

feet. They clapped, shouted, cheered and whistled. Undoubtedly, Dumbo's daring jump had made the show a great success. Dumbo blinked and smiled wistfully through the plaster, shaking his rattle. Then sadly, he lowered his head. He did not feel at all triumphant!

Later that same night, when the show was over, the clowns were in their tent removing costumes and make-up. 'Whew!' remarked one of them. 'Boy, oh boy! Did we wow 'em out there!'

'What a performance!' replied another as he climbed out of his robe. He seated himself at a table and removed his hat. 'Thirteen curtain calls! Thirteen!'

One man with a red beard nodded approvingly. 'We sure brought down da house all right!' he laughed. 'Oh mama, did we panic 'em!' He hopped out of his trick trousers and another clown stuck his head up out of them. 'Ask me — go ahead, ask me!' He grinned at his associates.

'You said it . . . we rolled 'em in the aisles!'

A clown in a bright green suit laughed and clapped his hands delightedly. 'Yeah! Boy, oh boy . . . what an act!'

'Oh . . . wotta act is right!' A huge clown dressed in an inflated suit strolled over to a mirror and pulled a plug from the centre of his back. The suit deflated like a balloon with the air let out. 'Stupendous . . . yeah . . . stupendous I calls it!'

The clown in the elephant mask removed the head. 'They'll have more respect for us clowns now,' he muttered.

'Boy, you said it!' One of the men dived into an open trunk and came up with a bottle. 'Here, boys . . . this calls for a real celebration!' He uncorked the bottle amidst cheers. 'Come and get it!' The clowns moved forward with their drinking cups. 'Am I thirsty!' said the first man in line, quickly downing his drink.

'I could use one of dem myself!' The elephant clown ran forward yelling, 'Dis one's on Dumbo!'

'Yeah . . . Dumbo!' echoed the man with a bottle that was almost empty.

'Dumbo,' called the others, raising their cups above their heads. With gusto they drank, then amidst merriment, queued to replenish their cups.

Outside their tent, little Dumbo was sitting beside a wash tub full of soapy water, and crying bitterly. He felt thoroughly miserable. Tim, the lovable mouse and the only friend he had, was washing plaster from Dumbo's head with a brush while he did his best to cheer up the baby elephant.

From inside the tent came another shriek of laughter as one of the clowns yelled, 'Here's plaster in his eyes!'

Tim stood on a cake of soap to reach some of the plaster heavily caked on Dumbo's trunk. 'See! They're drinkin' a toast to you!' Tim flung down the brush and gestured. 'Yeah . . . you're a big hit!'

Dumbo was not convinced — he didn't want to be. He felt wretched and utterly forlorn. Tim picked up the brush again and soaped it. 'Look here, you're terrific!'

Vigorously, the mouse scrubbed Dumbo's trunk. 'You're colossal, stupendous!'

Poor Dumbo could not stop crying. He was an outcast. The other elephants didn't want to know him ... and now he was ridiculed. It was too much. His thoughts made him cry harder than ever.

Tim jumped on to Dumbo's trunk. 'Come on!' he cried cheerily. 'Ally oop! I gotta wash behind your ears!' Obligingly, Dumbo lifted Tim in the air placing him on his head. 'You outta be proud,' continued Tim. 'You are a success!'

Tim's crumbs of comfort meant nothing to Dumbo. His tears fell like a shower of rain. Tim was worried. Laying down the scrubbing brush on Dumbo's head, the mouse swept off

his little hat and removed a peanut from the brim. 'Look.' he said coaxingly. 'A peanut! Come on . . . eat it! Got lotsa vitamins!'

Dumbo ignored his friend's pleas and the peanut. He just sat on the ground and tugged fretfully at a blade of grass. 'Give you a lot of . . . uh . . . pep!' said Tim, still proffering the peanut. Dumbo would not be won over. Dejectedly, Tim replaced the peanut in his hat. Suddenly he snapped his fingers and laughed. 'Ho,ho,ho,ho,ho, I forgot to tell ya . . .' Racing down Dumbo's trunk he turned round and stared up at his pal. 'Why, we're goin' over to see your mother!' Dumbo blinked his eyes in astonishment. This was the first good news that he'd had in days and days. A smile broke out on his face, and it was like the sun peeking through a damp cloud.

'Yeah, I made an appointment for ya . . .' prattled on the mouse, elated to see Dumbo perking up. 'Didn't I tell ya? Huh! Just like me. I musta forgot! Come on — get your hat!'

Dumbo reached for his hat which was hanging on a peg just inside the tent. When he had put it on, Tim jumped into its rim. From such a vantage point, he could show Dumbo the way. Dumbo rounded a corner. 'Now . . . right over there!' directed Tim from his comfortable position.

With guidance, Dumbo eventually arrived at the circus wagon with the sign 'Danger' on one side, and 'Mad Elephant,' on the other. Tim sniffed with disdain and disapproval. 'Cosy little place — ain't it!'

All was quiet. Dumbo approached the wagon and stood on his hind legs, raising his trunk towards the window. Tim, from his vantage point, peered inside. Raising his hand to his mouth he called, 'Mrs Jumbo!' He looked skyward, tapping his fingers. 'I hope she's in!'

Mrs Jumbo certainly was in — she hadn't any choice for her legs were chained. Her head was lowered but when she heard Tim's shrill whistle she looked towards the window. 'Someone to see ya,' cried out Tim.

Mrs Jumbo raised her head higher, looking surprised. Who could it be? She approached the window smiling happily. Really, she had an idea who her visitor might be and she hoped that she was right. After taking a few steps her chains rattled and pulled her to a sudden stop. For a moment she cringed back in fright, then she ducked and pulled ... and pulled, and pulled at them. It wasn't any use — they were very strong. But she smiled bravely and extended her trunk through the bars of the window.

The end of Dumbo's trunk felt around the window ledge. He was standing on his hind-legs close to the bars when suddenly his mother's trunk emerged. She felt for his head and caressed it lovingly. Smiling with happiness, Dumbo wrapped his trunk around

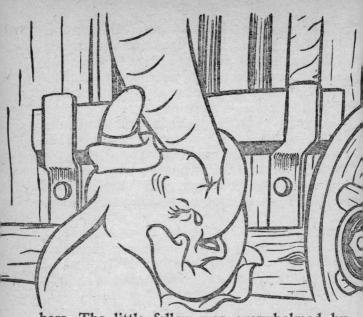

hers. The little fellow was overwhelmed by emotion and felt a deep, deep longing for the comfort that only his mother could give him. Tears flowed again as he nuzzled close to her. With a heart full of understanding, Mrs Jumbo formed her trunk into a cradle and coaxed her baby to sit in it. As he did so she began to rock him gently and sing:

Baby mine, don't you cry,
Rest your head close to my heart,
Never to part, baby mine!
Little one, when you play,
Don't you mind what they say,
Let those eyes sparkle and shine,
Never a tear ... baby mine!

As she sang her sweet melody, little Tim

stood on a wagon wheel with his hands behind his back. He was smiling and swaying in time to the music but his bright eyes were a little moist. In a cage nearby, a mother zebra nuzzled her sleeping baby; mother giraffe lay on a pile of hay clutching her baby close. A mother tiger lay with her twin cubs. One of them stretched and yawned, put his paws behind his head and moved, leaning against his mother's warm flanks. Monkeys rocked their babies too, and the newly born hyenas raised their heads and laughed, even in their sleep.

Hippos, ostriches, kangaroos, indeed all the other mother animals, clasped, embraced and fondled their sleeping infants. Tim regarded the tranquil scene from his wagon wheel perch and could not repress the tears which trickled down his tiny nose. He rubbed them away with his paw while the giant nursery listened to Mrs Jumbo's lullaby.

From your head to your toes,
Baby mine. You're so sweet
Goodness knows
Baby mine, you're so precious to me,
Cute as can be,
Baby of mine,
Baby mine . . . baby mine!

Dumbo was relaxed and smiling now but Tim knew it was time for them to leave. Gently, he tweaked Dumbo's tail and presently, Mrs Jumbo lowered her dear baby to the ground. Lovingly, she caressed him again with her trunk. Her heart was too full for words. Dumbo didn't want to let go — he clung and clung. But after a while and very reluctantly they had to part from each other. The baby elephant walked slowly away looking back over his shoulder, his eyes filled with longing.

Mrs Jumbo remained in the same position waving her trunk in an arc of farewell until Dumbo was far away from the wagon where she was imprisoned. When she could no longer hear the sound of his retreating steps she moved sadly back to her corner. Her kindly eyes were brimming with tears.

In their tent, the clowns continued to make merry; for them it was the biggest night of their circus careers. Never had an audience responded as they had this evening. The men couldn't stop talking about the success of the new act. Another bottle of champagne was produced and the men gathered round for refills.

A clown removed his slipper. Holding it out he called, 'Pour the champagne in me slipper, Joey!' Joey splashed the sparkling liquid into the clown's container, saying, 'Boy . . . I can't get over the way we rolled 'em in the aisles!'

'Just wait till we hit the big town,' piped up someone else.

The clowns grouped themselves closer. Amidst cheers one said with a mischievous smile, 'This gives me an idea. Let's raise the platform that Dumbo jumps from.'

'Yeah . . . yeah!' echoed the others in complete agreement.

In the background one of the men lay stretched out on a hammock strumming a guitar. 'Yes,' he said reflectively. 'If they laugh when he jumps twenty feet, they'll laugh *twice* as hard if he jumps forty feet.'

'Yeah! Dat's right. Dat's right,' cried the men in unison. The idea held lots of appeal.

Another clown seated on a chair waved his hand airily. 'Dat's right. Simple mathematics. Let's make it eighty feet!'

'Don't be a piker.' The guitar player stopped strumming. 'Hundred and eighty!'

From the back of the tent a clown wearing a funny hat and holding a trumpet between his toes yelled, 'Make it tree hundred!'

'A tousand,' called someone else.

'Yeah! That's it. Good!' were the callous comments.

'Hey! Be careful,' said one clown with more heart and kindlier feelings than the rest of the men. 'You'll hurt da little guy!'

'Aw . . . go on . . . elephant's ain't got no feelings!'

'Naw . . . dey're made of rubber!'

As the clowns continued their wild drinking spree, pouring liquid into hats, slippers, cups and anything else that was handy, their schemes became more and more rash.

'This idea's sensational,' came a shout. 'Let's go tell da boss.'

A clown in the act of raising a bucket containing champagne to his lips, grinned. 'Yeah, yeah, yeah! Hey . . . let's ask him for a raise!'

The others nodded enthusiastically. 'Yeah — this is worth real dough!'

Forming a line the clowns wove their way across the tent singing in loud voices:

Oh, we're gonna hit the big boss for a raise,
Yeah, we're gonna hit the big boss for a raise,
Oh, we're gonna get more money,
'Cos we know that we are funny,
We're gonna hit the big boss for a raise!

Weaving and winding in snake-like fashion
round the tent, one of them knocked against
an uncorked bottle of champagne. It fell into
the water bucket. The potent liquid sizzled
and bubbled as it circulated with the contents.

Meanwhile, Dumbo and Tim were on their
way back to the tent. Tim led the way, Dumbo
holding his friend's long tail in his trunk. Tim
felt worried. Dumbo's visit to his mother had
cheered him up for a while but now he was
crying again, crying as if his heart would
break.

'I know how ya feel, Dumbo,' said Tim as
they walked, 'but ya gotta pull yourself together. What would your mother think if she
saw you cryin' like this?'

Dumbo didn't reply but his tears fell even
faster. 'Remember,' said Tim, glancing over
his shoulder, 'you come of a proud race. Why,
you're uh . . . uh . . .' he struggled over the
word, 'a pachyderm! And pachyderms don't
cry!' Tim shrugged. 'What's cryin' get you
anyhow?'

Dumbo hiccoughed loudly, then hiccoughed again. 'Nothin' but the hiccoughs!'
commented Tim sagely.

Dumbo continued to hiccough — it seemed
that he could not stop. Tim looked round. Just
inside the entrance to the clown's tent, he
spotted the water bucket. There were cracks

in the wood and the water was running out through them. 'Well,' said Tim philosophically, 'Ain't nothin' a little water won't cure!' Taking the end of Dumbo's trunk, he led him inside the tent.

The clowns were all asleep and snoring loudly. A thin sliver of moon shone into the open tent flap, faintly illuminating the water tub, now partly filled with champagne. But of course, Tim did not know that. Splashing Dumbo's trunk inside the tub he waved his arm. 'Here . . . take a trunkful!' He dodged back as champagne splashed the rim of his hat. Removing it, he shook out the drops. Replacing his hat, he leaned against the side of the water barrel while Dumbo had a long drink.

'Listen, little fellow . . .' commented Tim while Dumbo drank his fill. 'We maybe had a lot of hard luck up till now but you and me is gonna do big things together! Hold your breath,' he advised, knowing that it was often a remedy for the hiccoughs.

Dumbo puffed out his cheeks like a pair of balloons. 'Why, your mother's gonna be so proud of you,' went on Tim. 'I'm gonna be proud of you, too. The whole circus is gonna be proud of you. Now whatta ya think of that?' Glancing up at his friend he saw with horror that Dumbo's face was turning red. 'Swallow it,' he yelled. 'You've held your breath long enough!'

With a mighty gulp, Dumbo swallowed the mouthful of champagne. He blinked, feeling peculiarly light-headed. 'Haw, haw . . . they can't keep us down!' said Tim confidently.

Dumbo hiccoughed again, but this time tiny bubbles floated from his trunk and danced away into the night air. 'Huh!' remarked Tim, 'I guess you had one tiny hiccough left over.' Dumbo sat down. Yes, he felt decidedly odd, but it was a nice feeling. His hat had fallen over his eye. He pushed it back in position with his trunk.

'Dumbo, we'll bounce back so hard . . .' Tim was still talking but Dumbo didn't appear to be listening. He hiccoughed yet again, emitting more bubbles. One of his big ears flopped forward falling over his eye. 'Hey! What's the matter wit chu?' asked Tim, scratching his head in perplexity.

Dumbo snorted, peeking out from between his ears and continuing to blow bubbles. With a grin he watched them float skywards.

'Say . . . what kind of water is this, any-how?' asked Tim. Climbing up the side of the barrel he hung on by his tail and leaned over the side. 'Oooooooh!' There was a small splash and Tim dropped in. As he swam around he took a good, long drink . . . then another . . . and another. By the time he reached the side of the tub he was singing. Leaning over its edge he laughed. 'Ha, ha! Ha, ha!' Then he started to hiccough. After a few seconds he managed to stagger down to the ground where Dumbo was sitting in a stupor.

The champagne had really gone to the little elephant's head. Each time he waved his trunk, bubbles poured forth. Tim, feeling rather tipsy himself, leaned on a bubble. It carried him up again to the edge of the barrel. 'Balloonies!' he shouted merrily. He caught the reflection of himself in an extra large bubble and reaching forward eagerly, hugged it to himself. 'Hi-ya, George!' he called to his reflection. The bubble floated upwards with Tim clinging to it. When it slipped from his grasp, he grabbed another bubble. He had lots of fun, jumping from one to another. Finally, he found himself sitting on Dumbo's head.

Tim slid down his friend's trunk and Dumbo opened his eyes blinking foolishly. He blew another bubble. First it was worm-shaped, then it rolled round forming a ball. 'That's pretty strick...er...slick!' said Tim, nodding approval. 'All right — let's see you blow a square one now!'

Dumbo puffed and puffed. A square bubble drifted into the air. 'Say . . . that's

very, very clever,' said Tim admiringly. Weaving and staggering, he prompted, 'Now blow uh . . . great . . . big one!' Proud of his achievement, Dumbo puffed and puffed again. An extra large bubble formed. He grinned, pleased with himself. As the bubble floated into the air it became a gorgeous shade of pink and gradually changed into a pink elephant. The pink elephant pranced sideways, stood on its hind-legs and posed. Dumbo smiled lazily, but when he glanced upwards, his ears flew out on either side of his head in surprise. Tim couldn't believe it. 'That's a pretty — hey!' his eyes popped in amazement. Were they playing him tricks? As Dumbo continued blowing bubbles, more and more pink elephants formed in the air.

'Dumbo,' shrieked Tim and, dashing frenziedly to his friend's side, climbed his trunk and hid beneath his hat. Cautiously, he peeked out. 'Do you see what I see?' he whispered. Four pink elephants had formed a line and were dancing, their trunks now becoming trumpets. Blasting forth music, the trumpets gradually came together to create a beautiful iris; a second later the flower exploded!

Fascinated, Dumbo and Tim watched the display. The pink elephants next formed a band. First, came the drum major, followed by two long-legged elephants playing trumpets, and then a very huge pachyderm clanging noisily on a cow bell. Several pink

elephants stepped on each other and angry
scowls were exchanged. The huge elephant
with the cow bell trod on a small trumpet-
player, who raised his foot to kick the huge
elephant. Immediately it turned into three
elephants, who leaned forward and trumpeted
a mighty blast of sound at the smaller
elephant. Not to be outdone, the smaller one
changed into a red elephant with yellow
cymbals, and the cymbals were transformed
into a whole row of elephants . . . the sky was
full of them. Amidst bursting bubbles and
tiny explosions, more and more elephants
appeared. They marched in long lines singing:

> Pink elephants on parade
> Here they come, hippity, hoppity
> They're here and there
> Pink elephants everywhere!

Suddenly, a bed formed in the air and
turned upside down. Flashing yellow lights
came from it as the song continued:

> Look out . . . look out!
> They're walking around the bed . . .
> On their heads . . .

The upside-down bed righted itself in mid-
air and a pink elephant peeped from beneath
the covers, gazing round in fright. It watched
the parade of pink elephants with surprise as
they sang:

> Clippity . . . cloppity . . .
> Arrayed in braid,

## Pink elephants on parade!

The frightened little elephant in the floating bed ducked hastily beneath the blankets and the bed swirled away, disappearing in a cloud of mist.

The grey head of a ghost elephant floated into sight singing, 'What'll I do?' Another ghost elephant hanging upside down replied, 'What'll I do?' And together they sang — 'What an unusual view.'

As they vanished, two worms wriggled through the air, one bright green, the other a vivid yellow, each carrying a parasol in its mouth. After bowing to each other, they took their departure, and a group of striped elephants soared into the scene. A world of fantasy, of charm and make-believe, of sheer magical splendour was revealed to Dumbo and Tim. Spellbound, they watched the bewildering display and the voices of the ghost elephants could be heard in song:

I can stand the sight of worms,
And look at microscopic germs
But technicolour pachyderms,
Is really too much for me!
I am not the type to faint
When things are odd . . .
Or things are quaint,
But seeing things you know that ain't
Can certainly give you an awful fright,
What a sight!
Chase 'em away . . . chase 'em away!

Still the elephants pranced and danced. Spotted ones, striped ones wearing red, green, yellow and blue — quite as brilliant as a rainbow. Some of them turned into great pyramids, whilst others became camels or waved their long trunks so that they resembled cobras. A swaying cobra revamped itself to emerge as an Egyptian dancer and was followed by a pair of pachyderms charmingly dancing a minuet.

The fanciful, absurd and yet totally wonderful scenes continued, as Dumbo and Tim stared with open mouths. It was strange, yet enchanting; like a play from the gossamer world of dreams. Leaping elephants dived through the air into an inky pool. A canoe appeared and a paddle which changed into a telescope. A white elephant rose majestically from the inky waters, took wing, changed colour and alighted on a skating rink. Other elephants glided on to the rink, and crashed into each other scattering brilliant showers of ice in all directions. Pink and blue elephants danced together, frequently changing colours. Sparks flew from their costumes and one enterprising creature used these as a filmy veil. As the elephants leapt in the air they landed with a heavy thud on the floor and were then transformed into cars. Soon it was choc-a-bloc full of all manner of swiftly moving vehicles — cars, trains, speed-boats, roller-coasters — and a multitude of waving flags.

It was a mad, magical world. Slowly, lazily, the last of the elephants drifted through the air and dissolved into blushing pink clouds.

Dawn broke in long streaks of light across the countryside, its first rosy blush silhouetting a tall, leafy tree.

Early morning sunshine had woken the birds and the countryside was alive with bursts of sweet melody. But in one particularly tall leafy tree a crowd of crows had gathered. Chattering amongst themselves in hushed tones, their voices conveyed an air of excitement, a hint of mystery.

High in the tree, a little crow wearing spectacles peered down through the branches. 'Well, looka here . . . looka here!'

Another crow, who played the role of preacher amongst his tardy flock, peeked downwards. 'My! My! Looks like this is most irregular!'

A straw-hatted crow peered beneath the brim of his hat. 'Well, I just cain't believe mah eyes!'

'Dey ain't dead, is dey?' The crow wearing glasses turned anxiously to his companions to ask the question.

Fat Crow closed his eyes, opened them and stared into space with a doubtful expression. 'No! Dead people don't snore — or do dey?'

The four birds remained huddled together

whispering and pointing to a lower limb of the tree. Their discussion was interrupted by the arrival of Dandy Crow. He dressed as a cowboy and enjoyed smoking big cigars. Alighting beside his pals he immediately forced his way to the centre of the group, saying 'Come on, step aside, brothers!' Swaggering, he added, 'Uh . . . what's cookin' 'round here?' Puffing out his chest, he drew on his cigar. 'What's the good news? What's fryin', boys?'

The crow wearing glasses said softly, 'Just look down dere, brother!'

Fat Crow pushed himself forward. 'An' prepare yourself for a shock!' Intrigued, Dandy Crow bent down and eyed the scene below. It wasn't an understatement by any means; what he saw came as a considerable shock.

On a stout lower limb of the tree, Dumbo was lying comfortably. His loud snores filled the air, combined with the snores of Tim who was curled up on Dumbo's trunk. They snored regularly and in rhythm. Dandy Crow clapped his hand to his head.

'Ahaw ... well ... hush mah beak!'

Straw Hat Crow strutted forward, challenging the others, 'Go ahead ... wake 'em up, bruther!'

Dandy Crow looked defiant. 'Yeah ...' cut in Glasses Crow, 'find out what they're doin' up here!'

'Yeah ... ask 'em what they want!' croaked Fat Crow.

Dandy Crow, full of his own importance,

brushed aside his feathered buddies. 'OK boys — leave it to me!' he said. Placing his cigar firmly in his mouth he descended the tree, landing on Dumbo's stomach. Puffing deeply, he blew a large cloud of smoke into Tim's face. The mouse began to cough . . . and cough . . . and cough. So much so, that finally, his eyes popped open. Almost immediately he closed them again. Dandy continued to stare. Tim's face wore a dazed expression. He opened his eyes again, this time more slowly, clapped his hands to his aching head and leaned back moaning, 'Ooooooooooooh! Those pink elephants!'

Dandy leaned against the trunk of the tree, his face inquisitive. 'Uh . . . Pink elephants!'

Ruefully, Tim rubbed his head. Dandy laughed. 'Hmmmmmmmm!' he said with a chuckle.

Tim glared at him then saw the other four crows above, also doubled up with laughter. Sitting upright on Dumbo's tummy, he glared at each of them in turn. 'What's so funny? What're you boys doin' down here, anyway?'

Dandy Crow jumped back. 'What're we doin' *down* here?' Turning to his feathered companions he said, 'Well — hear him talk!'

The crows burst into fresh peals of laughter. Tim waved his hand in a gesture of dismissal. 'Awww! Fly up a tree where you belong!' Laying his aching head on his arms, he wearily closed his eyes.

Dandy blew smoke rings round him. 'Say, looka here brother rat!'

Brother rat! That insult was too much for Tim. Indignantly, he jumped to his feet although his head was clanging like a bell. He pointed a finger angrily. 'Now listen,' he snapped, poking the crow on the chest. 'I ain't your brother — and I ain't no rat! See!' Tim and Dandy butted their heads together as they glared deep into each other's eyes.

Dandy gave Tim a push. 'Uhhuh, and I suppose you and no elephant ain't up no tree, either!' With another shove, he knocked Tim on his back. Tim shook his head, struggled to a sitting position and pushed the crow in return. 'No! No . . . me an' no tree ain't up . . . huh?' He broke off, looking shocked. Then he gasped 'Tree!' From the security of the branch he glanced downward, then gasped. Realisation dawned on him. He yelled — a loud, piercing yell.

Dandy Crow, highly amused, watched Tim's reactions with a broad smile. Tim ducked temporarily out of sight behind Dumbo's trunk . . . but not for long. Rapidly, he ran along Dumbo's trunk right up to his face. 'Dumbo,' he called urgently. 'Dumbo . . . wake up! Wake up, Dumbo!'

Slowly, reluctantly, Dumbo blinked at the light of day. 'Don't look now,' screeched Tim, disbelief still in his voice, 'but I think we're up a tree!' Lazily, Dumbo rolled his eyes, trying to pull himself together. Slowly, he looked left, then right. With a sudden cry he leapt into the air and crashed down on to a lower limb. He missed his footing and dangled in mid-air by his trunk. His weight was too much . . . the limb snapped and poor Dumbo hurtled earthwards.

The five crows clapped their hands to their

heads and raised their hats in the air. From
below came a very, very loud crash. For a
moment they all cringed, then gingerly they
leaned forward and looked down. The crash
was followed immediately by a rumble and
then a splash. Their mouths fell open in
amazement. Dumbo was in a deep pool of
water, his feet sticking up in the air. With a
violent squirm and a wriggle, he managed to
get to his feet, water running off him. Raising
the tree branch from the pool, he found Tim
clinging desperately to the end of it.

This amazing scene was too much for the
crows. They'd never seen anything so funny,
so hilarious — not ever! They laughed . . . and
laughed . . . and laughed. They laughed until
their sides ached and throughout their merriment, Tim was steadily growing more and
more annoyed. His fur coat was soaking but

he stood in an attitude of defiance, shaking his fist. 'Aw, don't pay no attention to them scarecrows,' he said to Dumbo, shaking water from his feet. 'Come on, let's get back to the circus!'

Dumbo climbed up the bank shaking himself free of water. The crows continued to guffaw — they couldn't stop. 'So long, boys!' one of them called cheekily.

Dumbo took Tim's tail in his trunk and together they marched, dismal and dejected, across a log. But Tim was thinking. 'I wonder how we ever got up in that tree, anyway?' he asked. Pausing, he turned to look back at the very tall tree from which they had just fallen. He stood completely still, scratching his head. 'Now . . . let's see . . .' He paced back and forth in a deep study. 'Elephant's can't climb trees, can they?' He shook his head in disgust. 'No . . . no . . . that's ridiculous!' Placing his hands behind his back he continued to think aloud. 'Couldn't jump up!' He immediately abandoned that idea. 'Uh, uh . . . it's too high!' 'Hey there, son!' called out Dandy Crow saucily, for he had been listening, 'Maybe you all flew up!' He waved his wings, demonstra-

ting a flying gesture.

Tim strode along the ground. 'Maybe we flew up ... yeah ... maybe we ...' He touched Dumbo's ear wonderingly then grew very excited. 'The very things that held you down,' he said, jumping jubilantly into the air and standing straight on his tail, 'are going to carry you up ... and up ... and up!' Dropping to the ground, for he didn't stand on his tail too often, he clutched his hands in wild excitement. Could it be — could it possibly be?

Wide-eyed he exclaimed, 'I can see it all now!' Taking hold of one of Dumbo's magnificent long ears he said with enthusiasm, 'I can see it all now!' Flinging his arms dramatically in the air he continued, 'Dumbo! The ninth wonder of the universe. The world's only flying elephant!' Excitedly he stood on his toes. From their perch in the tree, the crows continued to watch ... and again they doubled up with laughter. It was proving an entertaining morning for them.

The bespectacled crow hopped down onto the ground. Looking up at his comrades he called, 'Did you ever see an elephant fly?' He flew up to join his feathered friends with a squawk.

Preacher Crow spoke. 'Well, I've seen a horse fly!'

Fat Crow, sitting on a fence, flapped his wings. 'Ha! I've seen a dragon fly!'

Straw Hat Crow was lying on the limb of a tree, his hat covering his eyes. He tilted it back. 'Aheh ...' he shrugged, 'I've seen a house fly!' He laughed loudly at his joke and pulled his hat down over his eyes again.

Dandy Crow, now leaning nonchalantly against a fence post, took his long cigar from his mouth, knocking off the ashes. He strutted across the rail of the fence.

> Say! I seen all dat, too!
> I seen a peanut stand
> And heard a rubber band!
> I seen a needle that
> Winked its eye!

Pausing, he winked and hopped up to the top of the post, one wing crossed over his breast. Raising his hat, he continued:

> But I be done seen about everything,
> When I see uh elephant fly!
> What you say, boss?
> I said ... When I see uh elephant fly!

Tim glared angrily at Dandy Crow but Dandy was enjoying himself. He floated past Dumbo's head, flapped his wings beside his ears, then carried on:

> I've seen a front porch swing,
> Heard a diamond ring,
> I seen a polka dot railroad tie!
> But I be done seen about everything,
> When I see an elephant fly!

Tim looked disgusted but the other crows were enjoying Dandy's performance. The crow wearing glasses started to dance and make a sound like an ocarina; two of the others strutted up and down the fence. One called to the other, 'I saw a clothes horse arar' up and buck!' His friend nodded. 'And they tell me that a man made a vegetable truck!'

All the crows brought their heads together, each taking a turn to sing a line of the song:

I didn't see dat — I only heard!
Just to be sociable I'll take your word!
I heard a fireside chat!
I saw a baseball bat!
I just laughed till I thought I'd die!
But I be done seen about everything,
When I see uh elephant fly!
But I be done seen about everything
When I see uh elephant fly!
Fly, Fly, Fly!
Wid de wind . . .
When I see uh elephant fly!

All the time the crows sang, they broke apart to cavort, strut, dance, shuffle and play-act. They were having fun — great fun. But Tim grew angrier by the second and the sight of Dumbo's melancholy face almost made him choke with fury. Stomping across the ground he threw his cap down on a tree stump. 'All right . . . you wise birds!' He glared at the crows. 'This has gone far enough!'

The crows laughed again, their mirth increasing. To them, the situation was too funny. Dandy Crow leaned against a rock, drew deep on his cigar and said, 'Quiet, gentlemen! The reverend rodent is gonna address you!'

With an effort, Tim composed himself. He was determined to say his piece. He took a deep breath. 'You oughta be ashamed of yourselves. A bunch of big guys like you . . . pickin' on a poor little orphan like him!' Tim waved his arms in Dumbo's direction. The crows stopped laughing, perched on the fence and listened. Tim went on, 'Suppose you was torn away from your mother when you was a baby! Nobody to tuck you in at night, no warm soft caressing trunk to snuzzle into.' Tim paused, a tear dropping from his eye as he made an imaginary cradle of his arms.

The crows blinked, lowering their heads. Tim was making the picture very real. From the stump of a tree, Tim continued, 'How would you like to be left alone in the cold, cruel, heartless world?'

The bespectacled crow and Straw Hat Crow exchanged guilty glances. 'And why, I ask ya,' said Tim, 'Why? Just because he's got those big ears they call him a freak . . . the laughing stock of the circus. Then when his mudder tried to protect him . . . dey threw her into da clink!'

Dandy Crow looked down at the butt of his cigar, a hangdog expression on his face. A solitary tear dropped from his eye. Tim's appeal was really getting through to him. The four other crows looked embarrassed and terribly ashamed.

But Tim was not finished yet. Expressively, he spread his hands in a gesture of appeal. 'And on top of that,' he said, 'they made him a *clown*! Socially, he's washed up.'

Preacher Crow shuddered and hid his

embarrassed face behind his wing. Then all four crows were standing on the fence, crying. Tim carried on pressing home the truth of Dumbo's story. 'Aw, but what's da use talkin' to you cold-hearted birds. Go ahead, have your fun, laugh at 'im . . . kick 'im . . .' Tim accentuated the point by kicking his hat in the air. 'Yeah, now dat he's down . . . kick 'im . . . go on! We don't care!'

Tim dropped his arms to his sides. He had finished his speech and made his appeal. Would it do any good? Taking a handkerchief from his vest pocket he blew his nose then walked dejectedly over to Dumbo. He had a big lump in his throat.

'Come on, Dumbo,' said Tim. Obediently, Dumbo clutched Tim's tail in his trunk and followed him. Disconsolate and downcast, the inseparable friends walked slowly in the direction of the circus.

Dumbo and Tim's departure was observed by the now solemn crows. The recent objects of their ridicule withdrew with dignity, and yet there was a quality of pathos in the two figures retracing their footsteps towards the circus. Dandy Crow was the first one to recover from a sense of shock.

Hopping along the ground excitedly, he called out to Tim. 'Hey brother, wait a minute! Wait a minute! Don't go way feelin' like dat!'

Dumbo and Tim paused as Dandy caught up with them. Taking his cigar from his mouth, the bird put his wing around Tim. 'We done seen da light. You boys is OK.'

Tim drew sharply away, waving Dandy aside. 'Please, you've done enough!' Scowling, Tim stomped forward but Dandy Crow was not to be put off. He followed Dumbo and Tim, saying, 'Well . . . but we's all fixin' to help ya!'

Dumbo sat down and listened. Offers of help didn't come every day. The other crows were now in a huddle nearby, only too anxious to make amends for their unkind behaviour. Dandy had captured Dumbo and Tim's interest — he was going to make the most of the opportunity. Reaching round the back of Glasses Crow he yanked a long feather from his tail, causing the bird to jump in the air with a loud yell and rub his bottom. Dandy's unexpected action caused the crow's glasses to slide down his nose and onto the ground.

Dandy Crow spoke to Tim with a humorous twinkle in his eye. 'And den right after dat . . . you . . . uh . . . use the magic feather!' As he spoke those spell-binding words he produced the feather for Dumbo to see. Dandy knew that Tim was a very smart mouse so bending over him with a wink, he said, 'Ketch on?'

Tim caught on — very fast. If Dumbo could be persuaded that the feather really did have magical properties, he would attempt to fly with supreme confidence, not realising that it was his own magnificent ears actually doing the work. Gratefully, Tim accepted the feather. 'The magic feather . . . yeah, I gotcha!' Poking Dandy Crow with his elbow he winked back at his co-conspirator. Then he broke away from the huddle of crows and rushed towards Dumbo.

'Dumbo,' he called excitedly, 'Look. Have I got it!' He held the feather above his head. Dumbo gazed at it, a question in his shiny little eyes. 'The magic feather . . . it's the magic feather! Now, you can fly!' Tim jumped on Dumbo's trunk, tucked the feather in it then leapt back to the ground. Dumbo squinted down at the feather and gradually a big smile lit up his face.

Within a very short time, Dumbo was standing on the edge of a cliff, ready to receive his first flying lesson. Tim was perched on his hat supervising the action, the feather firmly tucked into Dumbo's trunk. The five crows were watching, more than anxious to see the baby elephant succeed. But getting him airborne presented a major problem. The crows grouped themselves behind Dumbo, pushing and shoving in unison. 'Let's go! Heave ho!' yelled the crows from behind.

Tim jumped up and down on Dumbo's trunk, frantically waving his arms. 'Come on now . . . up, down . . . up, down . . . one, two, one, two, one, two . . . faster! Faster . . . get up flying speed.' Dumbo flapped his ears raising a huge cloud of dust. Tim dashed back to his

position on Dumbo's head, continuing his instructions. 'Retract your landing gear . . . raise your fuselage!' The crows backed away as the dust grew even thicker, almost hiding Dumbo from view. 'Take off!' yelled Tim above the commotion. 'Take off!'

'Aw, it's no use, Dumbo.' Tim, almost choked by dust, raised one hand in the air. It was hopeless . . . or so it seemed. Wearily he sat down and leant his chin on his hands. Was his dream for Dumbo's success to remain but a dream?

Suddenly he jumped to his feet, thoroughly startled. His words almost tumbled over themselves in his excitement. 'Look! Look!' he shrieked. 'Hot diggity! You're flying! You're flying!' It seemed incredible, but the dream *had* come true. In the clear golden sunlight a moving shadow was reflected on the fields below — the shadow of Dumbo, the flying elephant. It was a thrilling never-to-be-forgotten moment . . . a moment of pure joy . . . of victory! Dumbo's face creased into a huge smile as he flapped his ears.

The crows who had been watching from the cliff's edge, laughed with joy and relief. Dandy's plan had been a success. Rapidly, they flew into the air to join Dumbo and Tim. Their laughter was jovial now. 'Ha! Ha! Ha! Ha!' said one of them admiringly. 'Why, he flies just like an eagle!'

The other crows chuckled. 'Better than an airplane!'

'Well, now I done seen everything!' shrieked Dandy.

The crows flew in formation above Dumbo's head, singing as they winged through the air. 'Well, I done seen about everything, when I see uh elephant fly!'

'Wid de wind!' called Fat Crow.

'When I see uh elephant fly,' continued the crows in chorus as they landed on some telephone wires. Dumbo flew in for a landing; the wires sagged as he alighted on them. The crows crowded in and perched themselves on Dumbo's head. The little elephant was elated. He had done it . . . he had proved that he *could* fly.

'Dumbo,' said Tim proudly. 'I knew you could do it! Wait'll we get to the big town!' Tim made an OK sign, smiling broadly at Dandy Crow. The idea of a magic feather had worked . . . with terrific results.

Dandy Crow, still clutching his cigar, flung his arms in the air. 'Boy! The city folks is sure in for a surprise!'

Everyone laughed as they pictured the sheer amazement that would greet Dumbo's startling performance. The crows showered hearty congratulations on Dumbo and wished him and little Tim the best of luck. Then with a big wave, they flew back to their favourite tree.

Dumbo and Tim returned jubilantly to the circus. Late that night when the crowds were assembled it was time for Dumbo to play his part as a baby clown trapped on the top of the burning building. No one at the circus knew Dumbo's wonderful secret and Tim and the elephant hugged themselves with secret delight. The big surprise would come later . . . at the end of the show.

To encourage Dumbo, Tim had decided to go on with him. The act went as before, with the firemen dashing about below and the clown dressed as a woman with the elephant mask shrieking, 'Oooooh! Oh, my baby!'

Far below, the firemen held out the safety net urging Dumbo, 'Come on, jump! Come on, jump!' Tim was perched on the end of Dumbo's trunk close to the feather. 'Come along . . . jump! Jump!' The firemen continued to shout while the audience waited with open mouths and wide eyes. Tim looked down at the huge crowd.

'Look at that house!' Dumbo followed his gaze, blinking happily. How different he felt to the last time that he had been perched on the top of the blazing building. 'Dumbo,' said Tim proudly. 'You're standing on the threshold of success!'

Dumbo glanced down again. 'Don't keep lookin' down — it'll make ya dizzy!' warned Tim. 'Boy, are they in for a surprise. Ho ho!' He held up his hand. 'Got the magic feather?' Dumbo nodded and winked.

In the ring below, drums were beating a dramatic roll of swelling sound to bring home to the audience the drama and daring of Dumbo's mighty leap to safety. As the spotlight moved through the air and centred on Dumbo, the crowd were silent with awe.

Tim dashed up Dumbo's trunk and perched in his hat. 'OK!' he yelled above the din. 'Contact! Take off!'

Dumbo leapt from the ledge . . . down . . . down . . . down the side of the burning building. The audience gasped. But suddenly the rush of wind caused by Dumbo's leap whipped the feather out of his trunk . . . away . . . away into the distance. Immediately, Dumbo's confidence turned to panic. He was convinced that without his magic feather, he could not fly.

'Oh . . . oh!' cried Tim in horror. 'The magic feather!' He knew its symbolism for Dumbo. Swiftly he slid down Dumbo's trunk for there wasn't a moment to lose. Dumbo's eyes were wide with fright. Tim looked up at his friend pleadingly. 'Dumbo . . . come on . . . fly! Open them ears! The feather was just a gag! You *can* fly . . . honest you can!' He folded his tiny hands in a praying pose . . . the

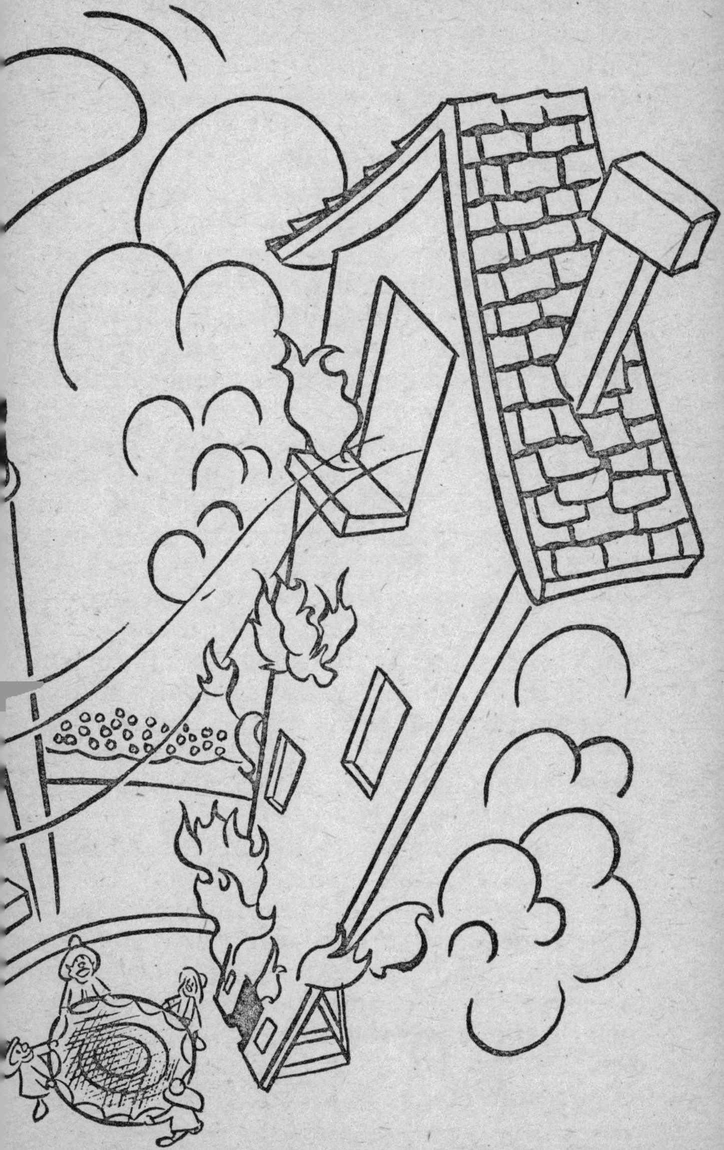

ring was coming up towards them at an alarming rate. He tried again. 'Hurry! Open 'em up!'

Dumbo seemed incapable of hearing — he was paralysed with fear. Finally, the meaning of Tim's words sunk in. 'PLEASE!' screamed Tim. Dumbo spread his magnificent ears and flapped them vigorously. Slowly but surely he gained height. A moment later he was soaring through the air, graceful as any giant bird.

It was a wonderful sight; but it was also a disconcerting sight to those watching. The clowns could not believe the evidence of their own eyes. Open-mouthed, they gazed upwards with stupid expressions on their faces. Dumbo flew right over the ring. The ringmaster, as dumbstruck as everyone else, dodged and ducked low as Dumbo flew in close. Right and left, back and forth he flew, every passing second bringing a stronger sense of elation.

Tim was enjoying the success every bit as much as Dumbo. He threw his arms in the air then turned a somersault on Dumbo's trunk, landing in the rim of his hat. 'Whee! We did it!' He couldn't contain his enthusiasm. He waved his hat in the air. Let's really show 'em Dumbo. *Power-dive!*'

Blithely, Dumbo followed his excited friend's instructions. This was fun! Down, down, down dived Dumbo causing havoc as he drew closer to the scattering clowns. They dashed in all directions, jumping into a barrel to escape. The last one in was rather fat and he bulged out over the edge, looking funny. A clown dropped a bucket of water, lost his balance and landed in the safety net intended for Dumbo. He went right through it and sat in the middle of the bucket of plaster. The other clowns laughed at his misfortune and he glared angrily as he wiped white plaster from his face and hair. He did not appreciate the joke!

Tim was enjoying the acrobatics more and more. 'Now . . . loop the loop,' he yelled to Dumbo. Dumbo needed no second telling. Over and over he went with as much skill as an aeroplane. In the ring he could see the clown who played the part of his mother in the act. Swooping low, he grabbed the elephant mask from the clown's head, causing him to fall flat on his face.

By now, the ringmaster was staring in fright. He had witnessed many strange spectacles in his role as circus ringmaster, but nothing like *this!* In a panic, he started to run as Dumbo hovered overhead. In his hurry he tripped over a large ball and fell head first into a bucket of water. Dumbo scooped up the elephant mask dropped by the clown and with great pleasure, dropped it on to the ringmaster's bottom which was sticking out of the pail.

Clown firemen dashed across the ring in their truck, smashing into the side of the burning building and leaving a huge hole in it. Quickly, they jumped from the truck and ran out through the gap. But Dumbo still had a trick or two up his sleeve. It was his night! Below, the peanut vendor was running away, pushing his cart marked 'Peanuts' as fast as he could. With pin-point accuracy, Dumbo swooped down and sucked the peanuts into his trunk. Terrified, the peanut vendor stopped dead and clapped his hands over his head — his cart, rolling on, bumped him from behind.

The four elephants who had been so very unkind to Dumbo, turning their backs on him when he was filled with despair, were standing on the edge of the ring gazing upwards like everyone else. Dumbo came in at close range and with a well aimed volley, sprayed them with the peanuts. They screamed in protest as the shots went home. Tim raised his hands in triumph. 'You're making history,' he told his friend. 'Real history!'

Without the shadow of a doubt, Dumbo *had* made history. By the following day, news of his startling accomplishments, his skilful and daredevil feats were news across the nation... indeed across the world. He claimed the headlines in all the leading newspapers. People were thunderstruck, gasping with surprise when they opened their morning papers. Throughout the day and night, newspaper presses roared the extraordinary news; extra editions were printed as the public clamoured to read about the miraculous elephant. It was the hottest news item.

The *Morning Sun* carried the headlines, 'Elephant Flies.' The *News Bulletin* splashed 'Wonder Elephant Soars to Fame' over the front page. Yet another paper sought wider readership with 'Miracle Mammoth Startles World' and showed spectacular pictures of Dumbo in flight. Insurance companies felt that such a rarity as a flying elephant called for special precautions so some papers advertised, 'Ears Insured for One Million Dollars' and carried a photo of Dumbo wearing an aviator's cap and dollar bills on his ears.

News flashes continued. 'Dumbo Sets Altitude Record' — Dumbo was shown with his cap held firmly in his trunk. Never, *never*, had an elephant been showered with so much publicity. As the days went by, Dumbo continued to be red hot news and regarded as very special property. He was presented with a silver cup for holding the altitude record. One newspaper went as far as to splash their front page with a headline 'Dumbombers for Defence' and show a formation of aeroplanes, all resembling Dumbo.

But the zenith, the real crest of the wave was reached when the *National Economy* magazine showed pictures of Tim, a very proud mouse, standing with a feather pen in his hand. He had just signed a highly important contract with a splendid flourish. His signature was bold: 'Timothy Q. Mouse.' The caption at the top of the contract read: 'Dumbo's Manager Signs Hollywood Contract!' That really was the cream — the *creme de la creme!*

During this time, Dumbo's days flowed past in a flurry of excitement and great activity. Everyone loved him now. He was a firm favourite — the darling of everyone's eye. It was a far cry from the misery of his earlier days. Fortune was smiling and a new journey was about to begin. There was a song in Dumbo's heart.

There was also a song in Casey Junior's whistle. The bright little train was bedecked with flowers for it was going to be its proud

duty to carry Dumbo, Mrs Jumbo, Tim and
others to Hollywood, the enchanted city. The
weather fitted the mood as the sun sparkled
and shone with dazzling splendour. The air
was fragrant with the scent of flowers and
promised more glorious days to come. At last
Casey Junior was ready to depart and it set off
along the shining tracks, singing merrily as it
wound its way across the countryside:

> I've seen a peanut stand,
> And heard a rubber band,
> I've seen a needle that winked its eye,
> But I be done seen everything,
> When I see uh elephant fly!
> When I see uh elephant fly!'

As the song filled the bright morning air,
elephants in the compartments waved their
trunks in rhythm with the music. Dumbo, now
an important celebrity, had his own stream-
lined car. In huge red letters the word
DUMBO was painted along its side.

Dear Mrs Jumbo no longer had to suffer
indignities, humiliation and disgrace. She had
been raised to a well-deserved and befitting
status. A very proud mother, she sat with the
elegance of a lady in a comfortable seat on the
platform of the observation car. Gracefully,
she waved a wispy handkerchief at cheering
onlookers. For her, it was an overwhelming
moment and compensated for the tragedy of
the past weeks. Anxiety, worry and pain had
dissolved in the glow of her dear little son's
overnight success. She gazed outwards, a tear
of happiness sparkling in her eye.

Overhead, Dumbo was flying along with the crows — his pals from the very special tree where they had discovered him. Tim occupied his usual place, close to the flying helmet Dumbo was wearing. The tiny elephant's face was alight with joy as he looked down at the world through his rose-coloured flying goggles. All the crows sang, Dumbo sang and even the train sang:

> But I done seen about everything
> When I see uh elephant fly...
> When I see uh elephant fly!

Dumbo flew down to the open observation platform. Skilfully, he made a perfect landing. His mother watched, her trunk extended and love gleaming in her eyes. Just like any baby, Dumbo slid down his mother's trunk and landed in her arms. He gave a little trumpet of pleasure and lovingly they kissed each other!

As the train chugged off into the distance, the crows exchanged happy glances. 'Hmmm ...' commented one of them. 'Look at 'im go!'

Dandy whispered softly, 'Happy landings, son!'

All the crows chorused in unison, 'When I see uh elephant fly!' It was time for them to turn back. Hollywood was not their home. Their home was the tree in which they had lived all their lives. Swooping down they alighted on a telephone pole by the tracks and flapped their wings in a semaphored wave of farewell.

'I wish I had got his autograph,' remarked Fat Crow.

'Oh, man . . . I *got* his autograph,' squawked Preacher Crow.

Straw Hat Crow stared after the vanishing train. 'Well, so long, glamour boy. So long . . . and good luck!'

One of the most beautiful books ever published~now available as a large, low priced quality paperback

THE ART OF

WALT DISNEY

FROM MICKEY MOUSE TO THE MAGIC KINGDOMS

# Walt Disney's Magic Kingdoms
## are available to you!
### With

**AMERICA and the world of DISNEY**

© WALT DISNEY PRODUCTIONS

This superb book - packed with full-colour illustrations - provides a fascinating guide to Disneyland and Walt Disney's World. It also tells the amazing rags-to-riches story of the Disney Empire, and takes us on a tour of the rest of America.

A UNIQUE PAPERBACK TRAVEL BOOK

# NOW FOR THE FIRST TIME

## *Walt Disney*

# SUPER 8MM HOME MOVIES

## OFFER THE **FUN** OF BOTH

# DISNEYLAND & DISNEY WORLD

## IN YOUR OWN HOME

### SPECIAL OFFER FOR NEW ENGLISH LIBRARY READERS

**✳ A DAY AT DISNEYLAND**

Here's a cherished souvenir that lets you relive the excitement and charm of Disneyland right in your own home! Enjoy a thrilling Matterhorn descent, Mickey Mouse and other favourite Disney characters, The World of Tomorrow, the fascinating Haunted Mansion, Bear Country and the delightful It's A Small World... a joyous film journey that shows why Disneyland is called "The Happiest Place on Earth."

**✳ VACATION WONDERLAND AT WALT DISNEY WORLD**

All the fun doesn't take place inside the Theme Parks—there's a world of family sport and amusement at the Vacation Wonderlands. Relive happy memories of the recreational facilities every time you show these films. Enjoy again the Polynesian Village, Monorail, rides, Fort Wilderness camp-grounds, fireworks and water-ski shows...and much, much more!

**YOURS FOR ONLY**

# £6.15 incl. VAT

## SAVE 40%

**ON NORMAL RETAIL PRICES**

---

# ALL YOU DO

*Walt Disney* SUPER 8 HOME MOVIES

© WALT DISNEY PRODUCTIONS

SEND CHEQUE/P.O. + 15p *POSTAGE* and *PACKING* MADE PAYABLE TO WALT DISNEY PRODUCTIONS LTD. TO:

WALT DISNEY PRODUCTIONS LTD., 83 PALL MALL LONDON S.W.1.

PLEASE RUSH ME:

A DAY AT DISNEYLAND ..............................................COPIES

VACATION WONDERLAND AT WALT DISNEY WORLD..........COPIES

NAME ............................................................................

ADDRESS ......................................................................

......................................................................................

......................................................................................